RACHEL KENLEY

Melusine's Daughters
Book One

WAVES OF
Pleasure

For more information contact:
Riverdale Avenue Books
5676 Riverdale Avenue
Riverdale, NY 10471
www.riverdaleavebooks.com

Design by www.formatting4U.com
Cover by Scott Carpenter
Digital ISBN: 978-1-62601-384-1
Print ISBN: 978-1-62601-385-8

A slightly different first edition was published by Ravenous
Romance, 9/2011
Second Edition June 2017

Dedication

For Lori Perkins,
who wanted a mermaid story—here's the first of three

And Mellisa
who reminds me to just keep swimming

Author's Note

Dear Reader,

As an author who has rewritten nearly ten different fairy tales, and edited dozen's more, I was thrilled to be able to dive (please insert short laugh) into the tales of mermaids. For this series I did research on the mythos surrounding these enduring creatures and I've tried to weave together several lesser-known tales of mermaids in order to fashion an original romance series with hints of the familiar.

After re-reading the original Hans Christian Anderson story, which does *not* end well for the little mermaid (in sharp contrast to the Disney version), the first story to capture my interest was about the split-fin mermaid, Melusine, whose earliest telling comes from France in the late 1300s. This is the standard tragic tale of a mermaid in love with a human who breaks his promise and loses her. Even with the sad ending, the character herself has a core of strength that appealed to me. She inspired me to write my own legend which is at the center of this series. As unusual as a split fin mermaid seems, a very familiar product logo uses Melusine, but you'll have to read on to find out which one it is, if you don't already know.

I have also borrowed from the darker story of the Rusalka. This water creature comes from Slavic mythology and is usually portrayed as ghostlike with haunting abilities. They occur when a woman or child dies violently before her time in or near a body of water. She is not allowed to rest in peace until her death is avenged.

One theme repeated throughout many, if not most, of the mermaid stories is one of trust. The mermaid doesn't trust the human with the truth of who and what she is. The hero breaks his vow because he is uncertain about the woman he loves, sensing there is something she is not telling him. When trust cannot be given, or it is broken, conflict arises. I believe how we trust says a great deal about who we are and what is important to us. Trust and love are closely linked, asking us to risk and be vulnerable to another person. Both my hero and heroine are challenged by this and must confront their fears to have their happily ever after.

I hope you enjoy Lyria's and Drew's story (and the ones that follow in the series) and that these tales become a welcome addition to the beautiful and varied mermaid pantheon.

All the best,
Rachel Kenley
Summer, 2017

Author's Guide to Aquatic Races

Oceanides, is a general term referring to all the sentient beings who live in the ocean. Unlike their human counterpoints, they have access to magic and ways to enhance it. The races can, and do, mix although the resulting offspring are not always accepted. There are several races mentioned in this series who differ from their mythological counterparts. The Oceanides are:

Mermaids and Mermen—Best known of the Oceanides. Male and female can change between the traditional fully human form and half human/half fin form. They can easily swim long distances. They live on land and prefer warm climates for their homes.

Rusalka—a former human who now lives as mermaid or merman after their lives were almost claimed by the ocean. This occurs when the human is changed by a healer at the time of death.

Kelpie—Water horse with ability to shapeshift into a human-appearing form. They tend to be born male which is why there is a fair amount of interbreeding with other Oceanide creatures.

Sea Dragon—The mixed race offspring of a mermaid/merman and a kelpie. The resulting race can shapeshift into three different forms: their bottom half into a traditional mermaid fin, their entire body into a horse form, or a combination of horse upper half and fin lower half. The last is how the race gets its name.

Lamia—A serpentine creature with the ability to be all snake/eel in appearance or half snake/half human. Not a particularly peaceful or diplomatic race.

Leviathan—A vicious and violet creature. They live in colder climates and destroy their enemies by putting the sharpened bones of their victims within created whirlpools and riptides. They are rarely if ever seen by humans, but they are the basis for many of the myths about sea monsters. They are squid-like in their natural form.

Angler Witch—Thought for a long time to be legend, they live in the deeper parts of the ocean where no sunlight reaches. It is not known how many exist. They are isolationists by nature.

The Legend of Melusine's Band

Long ago when the Earth formed, it was divided in two—the areas of land and the areas of water. Each was populated by a vast number of species. Those who came to rule on land were humanoid and they had no magic nor did they believe in it. Those who had rule over the water were the Oceanides and in addition to their shapeshifting abilities, they had magic.

For much of early time the two species lived separately, each vaguely aware of the other. As the humanoids increased in number, so too did they increase in violence. The Oceanides took to hiding themselves and their gifts. In addition, unknown to the humanoids and cloaked by magic, there were many islands and kingdoms where the Oceanides lived out of water.

It came to pass over many generations that magic was stronger in some Oceanides than others, especially the mermaids. While their men had some, that which developed in the women was stronger and more powerful. There came a time when the men sought to lessen the strength of their women and encouraged them to meet and mate with human males.

Although there were some strong love matches and marriages that succeeded, story has long told of how ruinous this turned out to be for both the humans and mermaids. After a time, however, tales of love gone wrong faded into distant memory, replaced by fear or foolishly forgotten completely.

One day a mermaid was born who was the daughter of royalty; she came from a long and powerful line of unbroken magic. Her name was Melusine.

Melusine's father was king of the merfolk and her mother came from a long line of the ruling class. Melusine was told from an early age that it was important she marry one of her own kind, preferably someone with the right background. Upon her 18th birthday Melusine was given an intricate golden necklace, thick and filigreed with gems and minerals from all parts of the sea, an inheritance from her mother's family. She grew in beauty, knowledge and magic, her strengths and gifts creating a time of great abundance and joy for her people.

However, when her father grew ill shortly after Melusine's 20th birthday it seemed likely she would ascend the throne unwed. Once word of this spread, the beautiful princess became a target for any and all distant male relatives.

Fearing for her life and freedom, the king set his army against their enemies, and Melusine fled to her private island and waited for word that it was safe to return. On a cold and stormy night, a ship crashed against the rocks near her retreat. She saved the men she could, one of whom was a prince. Using her magic, she cast them safely home. Remembering what happened, the prince went to the water's edge of his own home every day looking for the sea maiden who saved him. Eventually Melusine revealed herself to him, believing his actions showed a caring heart.

Sadly, she was wrong.

The Prince was an ambitious man, a third son, and not truly in line for the throne as his oldest brother was already married and had an heir. He had heard tales of the magic water creatures and once he met Melusine, he believed if he could win her as his wife, he would be able to use her magic to take over his brother's kingdom. He hid his intentions and wooed Melusine. Innocent and giving, she fell in love with the human and soon they were married. Her mother worried about the match, but her father was relieved Melusine would be protected.

So that her husband could be with her both in and out of water and rule by her side, she gifted him with a magic amulet. At its center was a unique gem forged by her magic from the three different sapphires she took from her necklace: the clear Stone of Clarity, the Stone of Strength which was a deep magnificent green and finally, the pink Stone of Love. The three stones together enabled him to learn and practice magic.

When her father died a few months after the wedding, Melusine was ready to lead her people and she was grateful to have her prince at her side. At her coronation, to acknowledge her husband as a co-ruler, she magically removed one strand of gold from the necklace and placed it around her husband's wrists. Once it was there, magic closed it so the band had no beginning and no end, as she believed their love to be. Outwardly the prince always showed support and found ways to help her rule even as he continued to make other plans and gain followers of his own among the Oceanides to whom he promised wealth and power once he assumed control.

All was well until Melusine gave birth a year later

to triplets, three daughters. It was then that the prince showed his true nature. Furious not to have sons, he locked Melusine in her room swearing she would be his prisoner until she bore him as many male heirs as she had daughters. He must have heirs if she was to help him take over his brother's kingdom. To keep her compliant, he threatened to have her daughters killed if she didn't do as he commanded. He told her that her magic, like her body, was his to command and she would do as he said or suffer the consequences. To prove his power over her, he tried to remove the band from her neck, but to their surprise it repelled him.

Still, she knew the band and magic were not enough protection. Petrified for her daughters' safety and horrified by her own unfortunate choice, Melusine meticulously planned her revenge. Each day she painfully pulled out her magic and imbued it into the gold threads of her bracelet. She ate little and hardly noticed what her husband did to her body. Growing weaker by the day, Melusine decided to do what she must to protect her daughters and destroy the Prince.

Finally, her work was complete. She waited for him to come to her that night and played the role he wanted her to play. She was soft and sweet. Offering words of apology and love, promising to do all he wanted, give him all he asked for. As he lay on the bed, she straddled him and placed her hand on the amulet which allowed him to live in and out of water. With the last of her energy, she forced magic through the amulet and shattered it back into the three original separate stones. Instantly, the Prince screamed, then began to gasp for air. Even though they were on land it was as though all the waters of the ocean filled his lungs.

Before long there was banging and shouting on the other side of the door. Her husband's final yell had brought his guards to her prison. Knowing these men were on his side and not knowing what they would do to her or her daughters, she did the last thing she could to protect her children and her kingdom.

Taking the three stones from the amulet, she wove them into the band that now held nearly all of her magic. Finally, she called back the thin gold strand that was around her dead husband's wrist and worked it into the bracelet where it glowed before settling into place. She magically broke the necklace into three bracelets, each with one of the stones and sent them to her daughters. She would give them her magic to protect them—body and heart.

With her dying breaths, Melusine created the promise of the jewels. In every generation three women would receive the bracelets. Each woman would have her own gifts which would benefit and protect their people. In addition, should she meet the right man, magic would show each woman her heart's true match. The bracelets must always be kept separate and always keep her daughters safe. However, should the day come that a great threat endangered her people, it could be stopped only if all three women worked together with the men who loved them.

The bracelets traveled through time, passed down only through the matriarchal line, from mother to daughter or eldest niece. Outside males and females tried unsuccessfully to steal them for the purpose of reuniting the three, for the power they held was unimaginable, but all failed.

It is said that each woman gifted with a bracelet

will lead an extraordinary life but must be careful to whom she gives her heart. Should she promise herself to the wrong man, the bracelet and its power and protection will desert her.

Chapter One

Point Pleasant, Jersey Shore—Ten Years Ago
Once upon a time….

It was her last night of freedom and Lyria wanted to spend it as far away as possible from her family and the preparations they were making for her 18th birthday. They may be excited for her to accept the role of Healer and begin to enhance her magic with the bracelet that came to her at birth, but to her, it meant she was trapped in a role she didn't choose, that she was good at only by chance, and which came with endless, unending responsibilities.

So much for the fun of becoming an adult that other mermaids enjoyed.

She'd swum hundreds of miles in the last two days, stopping at long forgotten or hidden islands to rest, and ignoring all attempts to contact her. She'd be back in time for the ceremony and celebration tomorrow. That was soon enough.

Initially, she didn't intend to spend any time this close to the humans. She almost never interacted with them, but she'd been drawn to this location ever since her first accidental visit shortly after her 13th birthday, the first year she was allowed to swim long distances alone.

She'd been watching the humans party, laugh and swim. Couples, friends and families. She could sense their joy and their enthusiasm. When people were here it was as if they didn't have a care in the world.

The sudden sensation of pain and panic drew her to the danger. A young girl was being claimed by the ocean. Lyria didn't know if she'd been swimming and something had gone wrong, but she knew without a doubt that the child was about to die.

She saw a man with a red floatation device on his back swimming to where the girl had gone under, but she knew he wasn't going get there in time. The girl was drifting deep beneath the surface and he likely wouldn't be able to find her in the dark of the water.

Lyria didn't think twice. She opened up her senses to the girl and the man, swam to the child and then did what she could to telepathically ease the little one's fear. She put a small gift in the girl's hand to help calm her, then poured healing energy into the girl, allowing her lungs to ease and find oxygen that hadn't been there a moment before. Finally, with her arms around the girl, Lyria swam to the man who was searching for the child and pushed her gently into his arms.

As soon as she knew he had her, Lyria swam smoothly away, not alerting the man to her presence. It didn't matter what the girl thought or said. All that mattered was her safety, and now that was assured.

Once she felt their energy received, Lyria peeked above the waves. Everyone was focused on the little girl so no one noticed her. It was bad enough the ocean would claim Lyria's life as of tomorrow. There was no need for it to take this child as well.

The ocean could be cruel and demanding. There were several *rusalkas* in her generation to prove it, their grief a part of them for all time. The thought of a young girl being burdened with that kind of pain her whole life broke Lyria's heart. She was pleased the man was there to help, since going close to the shoreline would have been dangerous for her. Without his help, Lyria's assistance wouldn't have been enough.

She liked his strength and determination. The first of those qualities she could see as he cut powerfully through the water, his arms and legs pumping, muscles bulging. The second she sensed as he came directly for the girl and pulled her into his arms. She was tempted to reach out and touch him, but stopped herself at the last moment, not wanting to distract him from his mission.

He piqued her curiosity, which was rare for her, especially when a humanoid was involved. Her vision was stronger than a human's because she normally looked at the world through the veil of water, and even from a distance it was easy to keep an eye on the life-saving man. A noisy crowd formed around the little girl after they got to the beach. At the center, a woman was crying. A mother.

Shortly after, the man left, but Lyria stayed close, hoping he might return. She didn't want to think about her reason why too closely, but she found herself curious about the man and wanted to see him again.

An hour later she was rewarded for her patience by the sight of him along the wooden walkway.

3

He was as good looking out of the water as in it. His tan skin suggested time in the sun, but sadness in his face suggested something she couldn't know the reason for. She loved his light grey eyes, the color of storm clouds, and found herself wondering if they sparkled when he smiled, darkened when he got angry. Or became excited.

This was silly. She must have seaweed in her brain. No matter how physically attractive he was, no matter how staring at him made her tingle, she needed to stay away. Even though it was tempting to get closer—it wasn't forbidden—something told her even one night would be too much. And not enough. As exciting as she found this section of land, she couldn't allow herself to be lured by the lights and the energy of the place.

Humans weren't to be trusted, especially men. All of Melusine's descendants knew this.

Besides, tomorrow her life would change forever and she'd be bound for life by duty and responsibility to her people. A human could have no part of it, and would never understand.

By the deep, even she didn't fully understand, but as the first daughter in her family, it fell to her to wear one of the bracelets which came from Melusine's Band and accept the role it required of her. As well as the loss of freedom that was part of the commitment.

"You need to come home," a familiar voice said.

Lyria was so caught up in her thoughts and despair she didn't hear her cousin, Amina swim up next to her. "How'd you know I'd be here?"

"I could tell you it was a good guess, but you know better than that. You know I love movies. I

4

know you love parts of the Jersey Shore. I think your secret is funny. You think mine is cute."

Lyria nodded and smiled. Amina did love human movies. She used to love to sing, but stopped that when they were children. Movies became her consolation.

She allowed herself one last look, took a moment to wish that her life could be different, then dove under the waves, making certain her fins didn't break the surface.

* * *

It was his last night trapped in New Jersey, and Drew Crawford couldn't wait to get as far away as possible from his family and this town which boxed him in to roles and expectations.

But first, he had a life to save.

The young girl practically popped out of the water and into Drew's arms. It was as if the water itself had pushed the drowning girl towards him. In all his years as a lifeguard, he had never experienced anything like this, but he wasn't going to argue.

"You're going to be fine, Amy," he said as he swam with her in his arms back to the shore. He was surprised by how relaxed she was in his grip. Most near-drowning victims thrashed even when they were safe continuing to be a potential danger to themselves and the lifeguard.

He still didn't fully understand how it was possible that she was alive, but he wasn't going to question his good fortune—or Amy's. She had been pulled out into deep waters by an unexpectedly strong

5

undertow, and she'd stopped breaking the ocean's surface by the time he had reached her. He dove under the waves, almost certain he wouldn't be able to find her in the dark water. He thanked whatever gods or angels were watching over Amy. She was damn lucky.

He had hoped his last week on the Jersey beaches would be quiet, but like most things over the last three months—hell, over the last 18 years if he was being honest—he didn't get his wish. The beaches and business were crazy crowded with people trying to get in one last summer thrill. The ocean, unfortunately, churned with riptides and stronger than usual waves, although no storms had come through recently. It was as if the water was angry. He'd blown his lifeguard's whistle more times in the last few days than he had all summer. He was more than ready to leave.

He couldn't wait to get in his car and drive off to Chicago where there were no boardwalks, no Heather, and no one who knew him or his family. He'd lived and worked in the Jersey Shore town of Point Pleasant his entire life and he was tired of being known as Sam's son, Michael's kid brother and Heather's boyfriend. Or, as it turned out, Heather's ex-boyfriend.

"You're leaving in the fall, Drew, and I'm staying here," she'd said on Memorial Day weekend. "You know as well as I do we've been drifting apart. There's no need for us to waste an entire summer pretending there's something lasting going on between us. I want to see other people."

She was right, but he didn't like her being the one to make the decision. By July Fourth, she was hanging around with some junior from a local college. He'd spent the first half of the summer hearing "Hey, where's Heather?" and the other half hearing, "Sorry to hear about you and Heather." At the beginning of August, he'd stopped going to parties with people he expected never to see again and picked up additional shifts at The Siren, a bar and restaurant on the boardwalk, to keep himself busy on nights and weekends. The money was better than lifeguarding and it would come in handy in his new life far away from here.

"Amy, we're almost at the shore. Just a little further and you'll be safe."

She spun around in his arms and put her hands around his neck as though they'd been playing together the whole time. "I know I will be. The lady told me so."

"The lady? What lady?" Drew was concerned. Had Amy sustained more trauma than he thought? Could she have hit her head? Been deprived of oxygen?

She opened her palm to show him a tiny hair comb inlaid with pearls. "The lady under the water. She gave me this when she brought me to you."

Drew looked at the small item in Amy's hand. He'd never seen anything like it, but her story didn't make sense. He glanced over his shoulder, just in case, to see if there was anyone else out there who'd either been helping him or needed his help, but he and Amy were alone. She must have had it with her when she swum out and forgot, or perhaps she'd been trying to get it from the ocean floor and that was what made her swim out too far.

There were no ladies in the water.

Shortly after Amy was safe in her mother's arms and enroute to the local hospital to make sure she was fine, Drew clocked out for the last time. His coworkers surprised him with a "goodbye and good luck" cake and a gift card to Amazon. He was touched, especially since he didn't feel as though he'd been connected to anyone during the summer. He knew he'd been remote the entire season, but many of them had known him for years, and he appreciated the gesture.

As he stood on the boardwalk and watched the sunset, Drew couldn't help but be a little sad. From the way he was counting the days until he left, it would seem he hated the place, but that wasn't entirely true. He had as many good memories of this place as bad, probably more if he really took time to stop and think. But he knew without a doubt that his future was somewhere else. He needed this change, and he'd been planning it, dreaming about it, for years.

"Hey, man, saying goodbye to the ocean? Think it will answer?"

Drew turned and saw Nico Vardini leaning over the rail next to him in an identical pose, although his friend had six inches and 50 pounds on him. "I guess."

"Your Civic all gassed up and set to go?"

"It is."

"Bet you've been ready for weeks."

"Longer," Drew said. "Couple of more things to put in it tomorrow morning and then it's me and the road to Chicago. You ready for the military life? When do you leave?"

"Right after Labor Day. Gotta admit, I'm a bit nervous. Still, given the choices out there for a dumb jock, it's a good option."

"You're not dumb."

"And I'm not much of a jock, unfortunately. Dad

still has the grumbles about the whole thing, but I think he knows it's the right decision."

Drew nodded. Nico was an only child, something Drew envied, but his dad didn't have the money to send him to college and Nico didn't have the grades for a scholarship like Drew. He'd chosen the army for its training and benefits. "Is he prepared for the change?"

Nico shrugged when he said, "Really doesn't matter if we are or aren't. I'll be home when I can and there are always people around to help, especially in the summer. Who knows? Maybe the old man will finally hook up with someone." The two of them looked at each other, then burst out laughing. "Yeah, I tried to say it with a straight face, but it wasn't happening. Still, Mom's been gone a while and I wish he had someone other than me. Think he'll see you next summer? The Siren won't be the same without you."

"Not if I can help it. There's too much here I never want to see again."

Nico didn't say anything. He knew Drew as well as anyone, possibly better, so there was no need for Drew to mention the one particular someone he didn't want to see again.

Sam, Drew's father, lived a life of perpetual disappointment in and annoyance of his younger son. He couldn't understand why Drew couldn't be more like his older brother, Michael.

Nico put a hand on Drew's shoulder and Drew appreciated the gesture. What a history they had. They were unlikely friends in middle school, Nico standing up for Drew when some bigger kids tried to push him around. When they got to high school, Drew focused on academics, which weren't Nico's strong suit, and he joined the swim team. During their sophomore year, Drew was so anxious to fit in with a popular crowd of boys he pulled a nasty prank on Nico in the cafeteria causing Nico to spend the rest of the day wearing his lunch.

Unable to live with the guilt, but unknown to the guys who now thought he was cool, Drew went to see Nico and apologized. He ended up getting a long talk from Mr. V. and became closer with Nico. They never acknowledged their friendship in school, where they hung out with different crowds, accepting the politics of high school. But all year long Drew earned money working at the Vardini's restaurant and bar, The Siren, and did it in addition to his lifeguarding duties during the summer. Any time he wasn't busy, he could be found there, whether Nico was around or not. Mr. V. was like a second father to him.

Or, truthfully, like a first, since his father, a contractor with a small company, didn't understand his younger son's desire to go to college and into big business. "Always thinking and acting like you are too good for us. You'll see when you get out there. The real world isn't like you imagine. You'll crawl back to us and beg for a job that matters." The 'us' being his dad and brother, who went straight from star quarterback, good enough for high school but not college, into the family business, making his father unendingly proud, something Drew could never achieve.

He was tired of being around people who didn't understand him or wanted him to be something else. He was clear about what he wanted and he saw it year after year when the rich tourists came to town. The expensive cars, summer homes, the big meals out. The admiration and calm acceptance and deference of total strangers. Clearly they had no concerns over how and when the bills were getting paid, or the stresses it caused a family. In the future he wouldn't have to wait to have something he wanted because he couldn't afford it. He wanted a life of money and class and seeing Point Pleasant in his rearview mirror was the first step to his goal.

Tomorrow morning he'd put the last of the things in his car and leave the Jersey Shore behind forever.

* * *

This summer

Drew dove naked into the ocean, as unconcerned about the lack of a lifeguard as he was about his lack of clothes. He may not have kept up with his certification, but he didn't have to worry about drowning. He was always safe in the Atlantic.

In early June the water on the Jersey Shore was still brisk from the winter's chill, but he didn't care. The warm air finally hinted at the summer to come, and he had been waiting to feel the embrace of the waves since he'd come back in March. He probably wouldn't be able to stay in it long, but even a short swim would be worth it.

He loved the salty coldness on his skin and reveled in the slightly illegal swim. Not only was it nearly 2:00 in the morning, but if he remembered correctly, skinny dipping was against some town ordinance. Somehow, when he was in the ocean he had no worries and anything that was bothering him seemed small and insignificant. The ocean was freedom and forgetting; two things he wanted and wasn't getting any time soon. Maybe when he was back on his financial feet he would start saving for a houseboat so he could leave land behind for good and live on the water. Or at least live closer to the ocean— just not in this area. He had lots of college friends who liked the West Coast and had moved out there after graduation. He could join them.

After getting out beyond the breaking waves, he flipped over and floated, allowing himself to dream of an unanchored life. No debts. No reputation to clear. New people. New friends.

Acquaintances. Friends were something he wasn't ready for yet.

He was enjoying the gentle rhythm of the ocean, letting it lull his body and thoughts when something brushed against him. He didn't think too much of it, assuming it was part of the undercurrent, but when it happened again and it felt like a stroke from his foot to his waist, he dropped into the water and came up treading.

"Hello? Anyone there?" Spinning around, Drew stared into the shadows, trying to discern shapes. The beach had been deserted when he arrived, but it didn't mean that someone hadn't come in after him. The moon was only days away from being full and since the sky was cloudless, it was easy to see for a long distance. When there was no answer other than the sound of the waves breaking on the shore, he stretched out on his back and resumed his swim.

The caress happened again a moment later, this time gently sweeping over his chest and directly to his cock, where it lingered for a breath before disappearing again. It couldn't be a wave. The placement was too deliberate, but when he lifted his head he still saw no one. He reached out beneath the water but didn't feel anything near. He'd always found swimming naked to be arousing, but this was different. If he didn't feel the Atlantic around him, he would have sworn he'd been stroked by a woman.

Clearly Drew had been working too hard and spending too many nights alone if he thought the ocean was trying to seduce him. He turned onto his chest and swam for shore. Even after years away and most of his time in the water in a pool, he was still a strong swimmer. Less than a minute later he was toweling off and trying to put on his clothes in the dark without getting too much sand in uncomfortable places.

He picked up his shoes and looked out at the water, enjoying once more how the waxing moon lit the night. Hopefully there would be another warm evening soon and he could come out again. He always loved the magic of swimming naked beneath a full moon. He shook his head as if to clear it of water. Magic. How stupid could he be?

The last year had given Drew enough indications that not only was there no magic in the world, but there wasn't a whole hell of a lot of goodness either. If there were, his business partner wouldn't have cheated him out of almost everything he had and destroyed his reputation in the process, Nico wouldn't have died in Kabul, and Drew wouldn't be working at The Siren again picking up the pieces of his life and trying to figure out how everything got so fucked up.

It was a short walk from where he swam to the

apartment he was staying in above The Siren. Mr. and Mrs. Vardini lived there when Nico was young, then moved into a house when they needed more room and business was solid. After Rose Vardini died and Nico left for the army, Mr. V. sold the house and moved into an assisted living residence saying he was done paying for landscaping in the summer, shoveling in the winter, and rambling around space he didn't need. Most summers the apartment was rented out for extra income, but when Drew came back to help out, Mr. V. offered the place to him and Drew accepted.

Even if it was above a restaurant and right on the boardwalk, it was isolated from residential neighbors. And from bad memories. Living on the boardwalk meant he rarely needed to go into town, which meant he didn't run into anyone who used to know him.

Especially his family.

He hadn't told them he was back and ended up having an unpleasant shock a few days ago when he discovered his ex-jock older brother, Michael, was dating his old high school girlfriend, Heather. When he ran into her on the boardwalk a few days ago, Drew thought it was a pleasant surprise. She looked good, if a little heavier than he remembered, and he was considering asking her to come to The Siren for drinks to talk and see where it might go, when Michael stepped out of the food kiosk behind them, handed Heather a fried Oreo, and put his arm around her. "Hey, little bro. Long time no see. Heard you were back."

"Hi, Michael. How are things?"

"Slow at the moment, but they're gonna pick up soon."

Drew recognized the familiar refrain from his

childhood. Knowing the fluctuations of work, Michael and his dad probably didn't have much, if any, business at the moment. Not that Drew was one to talk. As if on cue, Michael said, "Guess the big city was too much for you."

"Things didn't go as planned, but as you said, they're going to pick up."

"Sure, sure. Good thing you could come back to your old summer job, huh? Funny how some things don't change." Michael stroked Heather's shoulder possessively.

Drew didn't see any humor in it. He made his excuses and ended the conversation. He knew it wasn't going to be possible to avoid them forever. He couldn't wait for the run-in with his dad. That was going to be so special.

His hair was still wet and he was shivering a bit by the time he stepped into the apartment. As much as he didn't want to be back, he really did like this space. When he and Nico were kids, they would come up here to do their homework and play video games. Mostly play video games. It held happy memories and he was grateful for that.

He'd come back to Jersey with less than he'd left with, which was good because he drove a smaller car now. The black Audi TT was one of the only luxuries he'd been able to keep after Russell cleared out their accounts and left him with a pile of debts and no way to pay them. His liquid case was almost as small as it was when he was in high school. He'd sold everything but the car to pay off creditors and arrived in Jersey with a small wardrobe, his favorite music and movies and only a couple of thousand dollars in the bank.

Fortunately he didn't need much. The apartment over the Siren was furnished and had been updated and renovated a few years after Drew left. Instead of white wicker and hideous green rugs, it was now done in cool grays and blues with accents in silver and aqua. It made the place more appealing on the Air B&B listings that were now offline as long as he lived here.

There were two bedrooms and two baths all of which connected a huge living room, it was a perfect vacation rental. The kitchen was minimal and was fine for short-term renters. It would have bothered him more if he didn't have access to a commercial kitchen downstairs.

Drew put his keys on a hook, opened some windows to let in the cool night breeze and went out onto the porch which was more like a large balcony. He took in the view of the ocean and moon and wished, not for the first time, that they could give him an idea of what to do with his life.

* * *

Lyria saw him stand on the balcony and her sharp vision allowed her to see the pain and sadness in his eyes. She hadn't noticed that when she teased him in the water. It had been a lovely surprise to see him swimming and even better when she discovered he wore no clothes. Although she'd visited this beach when she could, she hadn't noticed him in a long time and was thrilled to see he'd returned. Since she last saw the life-saving man, he'd changed a little, but was still as marvelously sexy as ever. She couldn't resist making contact with him—he was simply too tempting—and Lyria preferred to give in to her temptations whenever possible rather than waste energy trying to resist them. There were so many things she needed to take seriously, so she took her fun wherever she could. He was definitely fun.

First she trailed her long hair over his legs. She needed to dart away quickly because he changed his position so fast. She'd been so caught up in his body that she'd forgotten he wouldn't be expecting her touch. When he began to float again, the moonlight on his skin begged for her fingers, and again she reached for him, this time with her hand. His skin was warm to her, even though he had been in the water for a while. She only needed to slip away a few feet when he searched for what had caused the feeling.

She was sorry to see that shortly after her interaction, he decided to go back to the land, but she was delighted to know he was here again. She took it as a sign from Melusine that this is where she should stay to hide the Stone of Clarity from Fiero, the Sea Dragon. It would definitely make her stay among the humans more pleasurable to have a familiar face—and body—to enjoy. It was fun to watch him walk naked out of the water. He had the most marvelous ass, which she hadn't had a chance to see years ago.

She'd been drawn by the sound of laughter that traveled beneath the water and the energy of the people who played here. Although she never had any desire to walk among humans, as some of her kin did, but she liked the atmosphere of this place. Even when the air chilled and the numbers of people dwindled, she occasionally peeked in on this piece of Earth to see and feel what was happening. Over time, she noticed businesses open and close, saw lovers meet and break up, and watched as the ocean reclaimed pieces while the arrogance of humans tried to push it back.

Because of her responsibilities and more recent concerns about the Sea Dragon, it had been more than two seasons since she last visited. When she fled their most recent battle, it was clear she needed a secure hiding place for herself and the Stone, which would have to be away from other merfolk. When an image of this place with its wooden lane and the lights as they reflected in the water at night came to mind, she set out immediately.

Diving under the water, Lyria fetched her scaled bag which held a few necessities for her time on land. Mostly clothes and a pair of shoes—which she hated—so she'd be able blend in with the humans. She swam to land and, as she got closer, shifted from fins to legs, ability all mercreatures possessed. She gasped during the change as a pain lanced through her, a nasty reminder of the injury given to her by the Sea Dragon earlier in the day. Shifting ripped at the skin and the wound was bleeding again, with the added discomfort from the salt water.

She walked onto the beach, enjoying the sand beneath her feet. Because of her injury, it took hours to swim here and she was tired and ready for sleep. Calling on her magic, she dried herself, slipped into the clothes, and walked out toward the businesses and nearby homes. There was nothing she'd be able to accomplish at this late time in their day. Tomorrow would be soon enough to join the crowds, and no one would guess a mermaid walked among them.

For tonight all she needed was a safe place to sleep. She reached out with her senses, another gift merfolk used since they needed to be able to communicate through the density of water, and found an unoccupied home where she could spend the night. Taking out a hair comb, she undid the simple lock and let herself in. She uncovered a couch in the central room, folded up the covering as a pillow, and lay down. Placing her hand on her injury, she covered it with scales, hoping the healing would be further along by morning. Here she was, her people's most gifted and powerful healer and she could do nothing for herself beyond the basics.

She was still close enough to the ocean to hear the waves, to feel its pull on her heart. As she closed her eyes, she sent a small prayer of thanks to the Goddess for getting her here safely and for the continued safety of her family.

The next morning, Lyria woke with the sunrise and stretched, wincing as the gash in her side pulled. She looked down at the injury. It looked improved, but she couldn't be certain. Breathing in the air, she tasted it for changes in the weather and found none. It promised to be a beautiful day, and while she was ready to do what was needed to hide the Stone, she was nervous about her next step. She'd never spent time on inhabited land before and although she was fairly confident in her ability to blend in, being so close to people who could not be trusted with her true identity wouldn't be easy.

As she sat up, the light caught the bracelet she always wore, the symbol of her importance in her community, coveted by Fiero, the Sea Dragon, along with two others. She held it in front of her, looking at it closely, something she hadn't done in years.

It was a heavy bracelet of woven gold ropes, threaded with various small gems and charms which had been added by previous wearers and imbued with magic. At its center was a distinctive white sapphire, the Stone of Clarity, sister stone to two others, the blue Stone of Peace, and the green Stone of Strength.

To anyone who saw it, it was a stunning priceless piece of jewelry, but Lyria knew the true price—a life in service to her people. It may as well be handcuffs. It wasn't that she didn't want to be a healer. She enjoyed helping others when she could, but her gifts weren't always enough, and when she failed, the emotional cost was high.

"No one expects you to be perfect," her cousin, Amina, said to her once when a young woman's illness was beyond her gifts.

"They don't mind if I'm not perfect for others, but not when it's their loved one. Can you blame them?"

"No, but they can't blame you either."

But they did. And she felt every loss.

And she couldn't ignore or escape the responsibility. The one time she tried to run away, two years after her bonding ceremony, Amina almost died from a reef stonefish attack. Lyria swore she would never leave her people unprotected again.

Even now that she was in hiding, she knew Amina could find her if there was an emergency greater than keeping the Stone from Fiero. Other healers had been alerted to the possibility of their help should the need arise.

Of course, Amina was in danger too, but Lyria couldn't think about that—or do anything about it.

For now her priorities was finding a safe place to

stay and remaining hidden, keeping the stone out of Fiero's control.

Lyria put on one of the dresses she'd taken from her island home and a pair of shoes borrowed from Amina, who loved the toys and trappings of humans, and she checked through the gold and jewels she'd need to trade for cash.

It was nearing 9:00 when she stepped onto the wood street for the first time. Even with the serious issues that had brought her here, she couldn't help but feel a thrill. The shops and stalls weren't open yet, but there were people running—although she didn't see anyone chasing them—and it was clear the place was waking up. Later it would be crowded and noisy. It was nice to feel as though the place was her own, if only for a little while. She needed time to get used to the location and being around humans.

As she walked, she saw an older man wizened by the sun and wearing a hat that came down almost to his eyebrows, sitting on a bench and throwing food to birds that surrounded him. Not knowing where to go to get the currency she needed, she focused on the man to get a sense of him—humans were easily readable—and decided he would be a safe person to ask for assistance. She joined him and he immediately offered her a smile and a "Good morning," along with a piece of whatever he was tossing to the birds.

"Thank you," she said, turning down the food. "I hope you don't mind if I ask you a question."

"Not at all, dear. How can I help?"

"I'm new in town and need to sell some jewelry for money. Do you know where I would go?"

"There's JJ's, a pawn shop, one block off the

boardwalk near the corner of Boston and Atlantic Avenues. They give fairly good deals, I hear. Probably open at 10:00 like most of the stores around here. Don't recall seeing any estate jewelry places about, but you could always check a phonebook. I think they still have phonebooks. And public phones. Maybe not."

Boardwalk, she thought. What a good name for the wooden lane. "I will go there. I appreciate your help."

They sat in companionable silence until he tipped the brim of his ill-fitting hat to her and walked, she assumed, home. She waited until she heard doors opening behind her, then gathered her bag and went in search of the shop.

JJ's was easy enough to find, but she dreaded having to step in. Her senses were immediately on alert, and she wanted to run. Before she opened the door she could smell the strong scents of old and battered things. The moment she stepped inside it was obvious this would not be a pleasant experience, but it needed to be done. Quickly if possible. The man behind the counter was as old and unwashed as most of his inventory.

"Good morning, pretty thing," he said, and she had no doubt he meant it when he called her thing. "What can I do for you?"

"I need to sell these." She brought out two gold cuff bracelets. They were both heavy. One was etched in intricate designs; one was inlaid with crystals.

"Well, I don't get much call for people wanting stuff like this."

"Then I suppose I will find another location."

He grabbed her by the wrist, pinning her where

she was. "No need to hurry off, missy. I didn't say I wouldn't take them off your hands. Just not sure I can give you what you were hoping."

Dismissive and untrustworthy, she thought. He had no idea how readable his face was to her. Humans were ridiculously bad at hiding their thoughts. "A fair price is all I need." *And to make a rapid exit*, she thought. This man was not to be trusted.

Of course, this was true about most human males, no matter if they showered or not.

"I could probably find a good buyer for the trinket you've got around your wrist."

Her hand flew to the bracelet. Not for the first time she wished magic could cloak it. No one had ever found a way, and she and Amina had searched different magical creatures for their assistance. "No, thank you, that's not available. Just these."

Lyria was glad to make it out of the store a few minutes later with only one nasty sexual proposition and enough money for a few days. As she walked back to the boardwalk, she looked at places to stay. From the prices listed outside, she had enough funds to take care of her shelter for the immediate future. She searched for and found a small place where the smell did not suggest she stay away and where the sign told her there was a vacancy.

It didn't take long to learn every corner of her new quarters. One room, a bathroom, television, and something called a microwave. She walked to a mirror, dropped her dress, and, after shifting the scales away, stared at the red raw line left by Fiero's magic. She'd never seen a blast like that. Water creatures typically shied away from powers connected to electricity, but this had the appearance of lightening, and sliced through her skin and scales like a blade. The injury started a few inches above where her fins normally began and extended for nearly three inches below. The blood cloud she saw growing in the water after the strike alarmed her, as did her continued inability to heal the wound.

How ironic. She was called for any and all serious cases and occasionally required to make life-and-death decisions for them. Unfortunately, she could not use her gift for herself when she most needed it. Instead, she'd required her Uncle Costin's magical assistant to escape from the Sea Dragon. Remembering her last minutes with them, she recalled her uncle's proclamation, which put her in greater jeopardy in the short term but offered the only potential for long-term freedom.

Lyria still shook with anger when she recalled Fiero's claim of betrothal between his family and hers.

"I have a contract signed by her father," Fiero argued. Where he found it, Lyria had no idea, but she recognized her father's shaky scrawl and apparently her uncle did as well.

"Signed by a male no longer living and not countersigned by the mother. It is not binding," Uncle Costin said.

"There was no mother or children at the time the agreement was made, which you can plainly see from the date."

Sea Dragons, the children of mermaids and kelpies, and merfolk had a mutual history filled with more problems than merfolk and humans did. The two communities were notoriously incompatible with completely different temperaments, and although the dragon population was relatively small, they were a constant challenge. Lyria couldn't believe her father had betrothed her to the Sea Dragon, although as a parent he had not been the most trustworthy of men and was frequently uncomfortable with the power of the people around him, none of whom where his family. Her mother married for love. To Lyria he had been remote, inconsistent at best. His death nearly ten years ago hardly affected her.

"He made a deal with my family when he was desperate for gold. The firstborn daughter of his family would be married to the eldest son of mine," Fiero said.

Lyria wondered if this was why her father often said, when drunk or angry, she should never have been born. Then she took it as proof he did not love her. Perhaps there had been something else behind his words.

Fiero continued, "To satisfy the conditions of the agreement. Lyria, is mine. That she happens to wear the Stone of Clarity is a bonus for me and mine."

Trying to remain calm, Uncle Costin said, "You cannot have her or the Stone of Clarity. I will not allow it."

"You have no choice. The contract is enforceable, and I will take it to the council. You cannot stop me."

"I can and I will. By the power of the seas and the magic and might of Aegir, if Lyria and the Stone are free three days past the coming full moon, they will remain out of your reach evermore." Lyria felt his magic course through her as he touched the bracelet.

Fiero roared with fury and let loose the bolt of energy that injured her. Her uncle cried out for her.

When he saw she had been injured, he helped her heal as best he could, then yelled for her to leave. The last thing she heard was Fiero yelling, "Hurry!" Lyria did not look back to see what he was doing.

She sent a telepathic message to her cousin, Amina, to fill a magicked bag with any necessities Lyria might need to stay on land and hide it in one of the secret grottos from their childhood. Amina sent no reply, but the bag was waiting for her. It was the only stop Lyria made before arriving on land.

She found some food in the bag—Amina always though ahead even when rushed—and ate while looking around the drab room which was, since land was better than water, as safe a place as she could think of. She missed her island home with its spacious rooms and walls that could be opened to the sea.

Feeling tired, she lay back on the strange bed and stared at the ceiling, trying not to imagine it pressing down on her. She would have preferred to have found a place more open, but the closer she remained to the humans, the less likely she was to be found. Mixing with their energy was the safest, if not the most pleasant, thing she could do. Here she would remain for the next six days waiting and hoping that on the third day after the full moon, she and the Stone would be safe and this nightmare would be over.

* * *

Drew wondered, why were the days leading up to the full moon always a nightmare? He'd been at work only a few hours and spent most of the time putting out fires, both figuratively and one literally. He was going to have to find a better place for the staff to smoke than the small alcove off the loading dock. They were lucky this time. He couldn't imagine having to explain to Mr. V. that he'd burned down the family business. What a fuck-up he'd become. It seemed not a day went by when he didn't notice something else he wasn't quite getting right. He needed to get out of here as soon as possible. Maybe it was time to get specific with Mr. V. and find out when the older man would be ready to come back. Mr. V. had taken a bad fall and needed to recuperate of his feet. When he'd called Drew to ask for help, Drew, who'd been staying on the couch of a college friend drinking most his days away, had actually welcomed the offer. That didn't last long.

Summer vacation was a few weeks away and while the influx of people would be good for business, he wasn't looking forward to the tourist season any more now than he had as a kid. He wouldn't see the beach much before sunset. Still, night swimming was fun, especially when you were visited by some sort of water spirit as he'd been last night. He'd enjoyed several erotic dreams after the strange encounter, whatever it was.

He finished unloading the day's food delivery into the walk-in refrigerator and freezer. At least the summer would bring in some extra help so he could hand off some of the manual labor that took up a good chunk of each day.

"What the hell is this?" From the tone, Drew could only guess what Stanley, one of his head chefs, was looking at. He hoped it didn't crawl. "We did not order these. Send them back."

Drew peered into one the crates that just arrived.

27

"It's dragon fruit," he said. He hadn't seen it since leaving Chicago. It wasn't something generally served in the restaurants around here.

"I don't want it cluttering up my fridge. Get rid of it."

"Sorry, I can't. I already signed for the load. We received everything we ordered. It must have been something extra."

"Well, don't expect me to use it or dispose of it when it goes bad." Stanley walked away, clearly annoyed. He had the temperament of a high-end chef and the range of a short-order cook. Not a great combination for a manager to deal with. Drew brought the fruit to his apartment to avoid any other conversations about it.

Yeah, it was a joy to be back.

Full moon madness was definitely approaching, and Drew was ready to howl.

* * *

Lyria woke from a short nap, stretched, and winced at the pain of her wound. She hated the reminder that the situation with Fiero required her to flee. True, she wasn't ready to face him, but hiding didn't sit well with her either. She looked again at the bracelet and the charms that dangled from it.

It was hard to believe something so beautiful could be such a problem and a challenge. The sunlight coming in the window created a sparkle, reminding her of the beautiful waves. When a cloud took the light away, it reminded her how fragile everything in her world was and how the simple could be complicated.

What appeared to be a beautifully faceted gem was also a source of great pain, and in the wrong hands, it could end or control the lives of millions of creatures.

She never wanted to be the Stone's guardian. Fiero would likely use it to give power to the sea dragons, possibly enslaving other creatures in the process. Not to mention how he would treat her as a wife. He'd probably lock her away as Melusine's husband did. Lyria could not let either of those things happen. Truthfully, she didn't know which was worse, although neither appealed to her.

But tonight she was safe and she wouldn't focus on what might be. Instead, because there was nothing else she could do to avoid either result, she would remain on land for three days past the full moon and keep the Stone hidden.

She fingered the space to the right of the Stone. It stood out on the crowded bracelet, but the empty area was more precious to her than any other charm.

"I wish I could have a bracelet like yours," Amina had said as they sat on the beach of Lyria's parent's island. "I mean, I know how it came to you and to Eden was horrible, of course, but still... It would be nice to be important."

She'd learned earlier at the presentation ceremony how her life would be scripted and directed because of a piece of jewelry. Rather than the band coming to her at her aunt's death, it had been given to her when she turned 16. The bonding ceremony would happen in two years. She had not been impressed with its sparkles or beauty. Lyria had hardly heard her as she fingered the charms. "What did you say?"

"I think you're lucky."

"Trust me, I'm not." Still, Amina had looked so wistfully at her, she couldn't help but smile. Amina was four years younger and had an older sister nearly Lyria's age, but she was always closer to Amina. The Stone of Strength was worn by Amina's sister, Eden. Amina often coveted what Lyria had. If giving Amina the bracelet could free her from her duties as family healer, she would have handed over the thing in an instant. But that wasn't an option. Still, no one said she had to keep it completely intact.

She'd stood and taken her cousin's hand. "Come with me," she'd said and the two had gone into house. Taking off the bracelet, and loving how she instantly felt lighter, she'd reached to the right of the center stone and removed a dangling charm consisting of tiny slices of agate worked to look like the leaves of a flowing sea plant. Knowing her cousin would love the variety of colors, Lyria hooked the link onto one of her gold chains.

"Here, Amina, bend your head down," she'd said. She'd clasped the bracelet around Amina's neck and continued, "You are now bound to the heritage of Melusine's Band, and we are bound to each other for eternity."

Amina had looked up at Lyria with tears in her eyes and Lyria couldn't help but feel emotional too. What had started as a gesture now felt like something of significance. Sunlight had caught the colors on the charm and shone into Lyria's eyes. Perhaps this, too, was meant to be. She could not share the burden, but for the first time she thought she might not be completely alone in what she needed to do.

It was one of her best memories associated with

the Band. She'd hoped for more, but until the third day of the waning moon, there was nothing to be done. Weary, she put the bracelet back on, shivering as the cool gold touched her skin.

Ironically, she supposed, circumstances had conspired to bring the Stone of Peace to Amina. Her cousin had gotten her wish, so they were bound by that as well. Amina, somewhat empathic as a child, was not the strongest empath the Oceanides had every known,

Lyria's stomach growled and she realized she hadn't eaten in hours. She wasn't certain what she'd find, but she'd always seen people with food when she visited and watched, so she slipped on her dress and shoes and joined the crowds on the boardwalk.

She loved the sweet smells and the laughter she'd heard on her distant visits, but since she had never swam too close, she didn't expect to be as overwhelmed and excited as she was. It wasn't the kind of life she was used to, but there was great beauty here and she let the lights and energy surround her and pull her along.

There were couples laughing, groups of girls and boys flirting with each other, and even families with children mixed in. It seemed as though no one was left out of the fun, no matter what they were doing. Giant mechanical structures pulled people high and made them scream with delight. Lyria watched people play at booths and learned some of the games that lead to squeals of glee and funny toys being handed over. Then there was the food, none of it familiar, yet all of it smelling wonderful. She tried something called Sicilian pizza and, after burning her lips slightly on the first bite, sighed with every delicious cheesy and doughy mouthful. Humans certainly had a knack for decadent foods.

As the evening wore on, strains of music drew her drew her to a club, which she found amusing since this was a characteristic assigned by humans to her people, and one of the few that was often accurate. She found where the music was coming from and had to smile. The establishment was called The Siren and seemed to be perfectly named. Reading the sign out front, she wasn't certain what jazz was, but the music playing was so enticing, she followed it in.

The place was crowded. Lyria maneuvered her way around the bodies, not particularly comfortable with their proximity. She was grateful when she found a single seat at a long wooden bar where people were enjoying multicolored drinks. She saw one go by with salt around the rim and decided it was something she'd enjoy. After asking the woman passing the drink what it was called, she ordered her first margarita. When the pretty concoction arrived, she took a small taste and was delighted with her choice. Cool, salty and tart, it started a tingle in her stomach she recognized as an effect of alcohol. Knowing her susceptibility to the substance—merfolk were not particularly good with spirits, even those who had a higher percentage of human blood—she made a mental note to drink slowly.

Continuing to sip her drink, Lyria turned to face the room and took in the sea of humanity. From what she could tell, the people were mostly young, some sitting drinking in groups or couples, others dancing on the center floor. Their movements were beautiful and often seductive. When Lyria opened her senses, she discovered the atmosphere was charged with desire, something that made her tingle more than the margarita.

She enjoyed watching them dance, some trying to impress the person they were with or attract the attention of another, some allowing the music to guide them. There was an unexpected beauty to the color and form mixing together. When a woman bobbled in her dance moves, Lyria looked down at her feet and saw, to her horror, the woman wore shoes with ridiculously high heels. Amina had a pair like that. She loved human fashion. Stilettos she called them. They did indeed resemble knives. Lyria's feet ached at the thought of being forced into something so confining. Flexing her toes in the borrowed sequined flats she wore, she was grateful Amina had packed something more comfortable.

As Lyria watched, her heart jumped in surprise when she saw the man from the ocean across the room. The Goddess continued to smile on her.

He was so much better-looking up close. Strong features were kept from being intimidating by a cleft in his chin and a dimple on the left side that showed when he smiled. In the dark she couldn't see their color clearly, but she remembered his eyes were gray. Tonight they were outlined by brows which were often drawn down.

Perhaps, Lyria thought, she could find a way to soften his expression.

Chapter Two

The combo was in full swing when Drew noticed the gorgeous woman at the bar. Her very long red hair was hard to miss since it hung loose to the center of her back with strands curling around her face. She turned, as if sensing his attention, and he was riveted by her features. Her mouth was full and lush, begging to be kissed, and her eyes were almost doll-like in their size. He wished the room wasn't so dim so he could see their color, but even from a distance he noticed an uncertainty.

He watched her sip a margarita. The pleasure on her face as she swallowed made him long to keep her pleased. It was the strangest reaction, but too strong to ignore. She wore a light blue sleeveless dress that appeared to be made from a material so thin he wondered if in the right light he could see through it. Unfortunately it fell nearly to her ankles. He was dying to see her legs.

He saw other men noticing her and, with a feeling of possessiveness he didn't care to analyze, he moved to introduce himself. He was glad for the noise because it gave him an excuse to lean close to her when he spoke.

"Welcome to The Siren. I don't think I've seen you here before. I'm Drew Crawford." He held out his hand and she slid hers gently into it. No businesslike handshake from her. Instead the touch had an intimate feel as though she were caressing the most available part of his body.

"I'm Lyria, and no, you haven't seen me here before. I only arrived in town today."

"How did you hear about us?"

"I didn't hear about you. I heard the music and came to hear more."

"You like it?"

"Yes, very much. It has a beautiful flow and harmony."

"We only started hosting jazz nights on Wednesdays a month or so ago."

"We?"

"I manage this place. The club and the restaurant."

"Well, clearly the music is popular," she said, gesturing to the crowd.

It was the most casual and pointless conversation he'd experienced in a while, but as long as her attention was on him, he didn't care. "So, what brings you to the area?"

She paused before answering and he hoped her reply wouldn't mention a man. "I needed some time away. I'd visited years ago so when I was looking for a place to disappear, this seemed like a good choice."

"It's still early in the season. Wait until schools are out and vacation season officially starts. Then it gets crazy."

"I can handle a little crazy," she said with a smile. The uncertain and distant look in her eyes disappeared when she smiled. It was as good a reason as any to keep her smiling. Unfortunately, business took the opportunity to intervene in the form of one of his servers.

"Hey, boss man, there's a problem in the kitchen. A clash of wills—or more like won'ts—again."

He shook his head. Drew's two lead chefs were at each other's throats at least once a night, more often if he was unlucky. He had come to understand the literal meaning of too many cooks spoiling the broth. Either it was going to be a long and painful summer or there was going to be a chalk body outline on the floor and he'd need an alibi.

Something had to change and soon.

Tonight, however, was not the night to do it. For now he'd calm the waters and get back to Lyria as quickly as possible. "I need to take care of this personally. I hope you weren't planning on leaving."

"I'm enjoying being here, so I expect I'll be staying." A stray piece of salt clung to her lip and she licked it away. Drew wondered if standing up without attracting attention was going to be an option. He flashed on an image of his brother and Heather. That cooled his blood.

"Do you think you'll be long?" she asked.

"Not if I can help it."

"Good," she said and smiled again.

He couldn't believe how reluctant he was to leave a woman he'd met only minutes before, and for a change it was wanting to be with her and not dreading what he would find in the kitchen that had him wishing he didn't need to run the place.

There was a time when he loved hanging out in the kitchen. Mr. V. was typically behind the stove cooking up favorites and occasionally trying something new. Drew learned food didn't have to come canned, frozen or from a mix, and Mr. V. taught as well as he cooked. Drew's kitchen skills earned him friends when he was in college and impressed women when he was out on his own. He was one of the only bachelors he knew who had something other than beer and takeout in their refrigerators.

Unfortunately, since taking over The Siren, he'd inherited more drama than he expected, something he'd never enjoyed and liked less now with a beautiful woman waiting for him in the club. Somehow he managed to placate both men, wishing he could send them to their separate rooms like misbehaving children. As he made his way back to where he'd left Lyria he was stopped several times, both by staff and regular patrons. Normally he didn't mind the meet-and-greet since it was good for business, but tonight he had something—someone—else on his mind.

Except she wasn't there when he returned. He barely managed to keep himself from slamming a fist on the bar as he turned to scan the crowd. But it took no time to locate her. She stood on the dance floor, moving to the music as if entranced, her dress flowing around her. Other couples and singles were also slow dancing, but Lyria was alone and clearly didn't care. She looked as though the music were inside her and coming out through her movements. The other males were showing great restraint if they all weren't hovering around her, and he decided not to take a chance on their restraint giving out.

He walked up behind her and whispered in her ear, "May I join you?"

* * *

Lyria was glad he came back. She sensed him before feeling him against her back. He put his arms around her waist and she leaned against him, enjoying the warmth of his skin against the thin material of her dress. She reached a hand back to caress his jaw and neck and felt the change in the heat of him, the tension in his muscles that had nothing to do with concern and everything to do with attraction. It was rare when she couldn't have a man she wanted and tonight was no exception. Of course, it was well known in merlore that human males were particularly susceptible to the pull of mermaids, and tonight and for the remainder of her stay, she was going to enjoy this power. Why not have fun while in exile if she could. As long as she remembered not to trust him or allow any deeper emotions to grow between them, there would be no long-term consequences of her pleasure.

They continued to dance with her facing away from him as though they were ignoring each other, and the sexual tension grew. His hand moved from her waist to her stomach and she swayed her hips in a circular motion so he had no doubt that his touch pleased her. She picked up on a few stray thoughts of the people around her: women who were annoyed she'd earned his attention, men who were longing for hers or wishing their dates acted as she did. Humans. Always wanting what they didn't have or what they saw someone else having, never noticing how much abundance was in their own lives.

As the music changed, she turned in his arms, wanting to see his expression, the desire in his eyes.

38

She could almost taste his attraction to her, how much he ached to have her in his bed. His hands rested on the curve at the top of her ass. She wondered what he might think if he discovered where his hands currently rested would turn to scales and a tail when she shifted to her other form. It made her smile.

"Something funny?" he asked, noticing her change in expression.

"No, something pleasant. Very pleasant. Don't you think?"

"Absolutely," he said and pulled her closer. He put his hands under her hair to place them on her back, then stepped away a little.

"What's wrong?" she asked.

"You're not wearing a bra" he said. His expression showed he knew he sounded stupid. "I wasn't sure it was okay to be touching you without asking for consent."

She laughed. "I'm not wearing anything under this. Never have, never do. And I like your touch exactly where it is."

* * *

Dancing close could be a bad idea, because it wouldn't take long for her to discover he was hard as stone. She took the decision away from him, however, when she pressed herself close and continued to move with the music. If she felt his erection, she didn't mind since nothing changed about her movements. Her head fit under his chin and without any hesitation she placed her head on his chest as though she'd been doing it forever.

She ran a hand through his hair, playing with it, and when she sighed he felt it as a hum against his body. "This is wonderful," she said. "It's nice to be wrapped up in both the music and you."

There was something bold and innocent about her words. As she spoke the simple truth, his mind flashed on images of her naked in his arms calling his name out in her passion. He couldn't remember ever wanting a woman as quickly or as intensely as he did her. It was a pleasant surprise to learn his feelings weren't completely shut down, or that his thoughts were something other than negative.

They didn't speak for the remainder of the song or the next one, but before they could enjoy a third, he was interrupted by another business issue. She continued to dance on her own as he listened to an employee apprise him of a situation involving a patron. "I hate to do this to you," he said, "but I need to take care of something."

"Managing leaves little time for dancing."

"On some nights, yes. Most problems end up with me."

"Then you must take care of it. If you think you will be back, I am willing to wait for you."

"I'll be back," he said, and on impulse he kissed her. What was meant to be a quick kiss became more when her hands instantly rose to cup his face and hold him to her. Her lips were soft and yielding and when her mouth opened on a sigh, he seized the opportunity to taste her. He noticed the lingering salty and tangy flavor of her drink along with something unique, something which made him pull her closer. As he did, he breathed in the scent of her skin and thoughts of waves hitting the sand entered his mind. His heart raced and his fingers tingled with the need to touch her. If they were alone, he'd have ripped the fabric from her body.

He'd kissed plenty of women in his life. His first kiss had been on this very boardwalk, not far from where they stood, but none were like this. Songs and romance movies were filled with the concept of the world melting away leaving only the two lovers, lost in their embrace. He never believed it—until now.

He was aware of her scent, her taste, the feel of her hair in one hand, her back on the other. The jazz combo sounded far away, his heartbeat drowning it out.

He surrendered to the feel of her, the simple utter joy of their kiss. This is what the final moments of drowning must be like. Breathless bliss.

Unexpectedly, she put her hand on his chest and pushed against him, ending the kiss. "Take care of the problem. I will be here when you're ready to take care of me."

* * *

Lyria's eyes raked over his body as he walked away and she smiled when he turned back to look at her. He was so much more fun and delicious than she'd imagined. She sent praises to Melusine for finding him on her first night, another good sign. She honestly had no idea he would be here. It was the music she found compelling, although not as much as the man.

As she lost herself again in the flow of the notes,

she thought about Drew, about what remained the same and what had changed. His hair was longer then in the past. She liked the way it fell in waves and the tracks his fingers made as he ran them through it in frustration.

He'd kept his swimmer's build, long and lean, with muscles in his upper arms that were sexy in the short sleeves he wore. She couldn't help but wonder if his legs would be as strong and how they would feel pressed against her during sex. The light gray of his eyes was less noticeable in the dark room, but their intensity was the same.

In fact, intensity was the dominant emotion she felt coming off him, yet he also seemed sad. She didn't have Amina's gift of empathy, but she could read people —merfolk and therefore humans—fairly well. Darkness and unhappiness lurked beneath the surface of this man. It made her curious. She'd never been as curious about a human before and had never wanted to take one to bed. Most of the men she met and enjoyed were like her, interested in fun and pleasure but not much else. If she discovered they wanted more, she never saw them again. She'd earned a reputation as uncatchable. Of course, after the disaster with Wilmar five years ago, she'd take cold over being used.

But there was something about Drew which sparked more than a sexual fantasy. Yes, she wanted to see what it would be like to pleasure and be pleasured by him, but she also wanted to know what made his eyes so sad. She remembered the yearning sadness in his eyes from when she had last seen him, but then she'd also sensed hope.

Ten years had passed and whatever he had done

and accomplished had not made him any happier. He still seemed lost and ill at ease. She wanted to change that for him, bring him the joy that was an inherent part of who she was. Even with her responsibilities as a healer, not to mention keeper of the Stone, it seemed to Lyria, she had more happiness and freedom than he did. She could sense it, feel it as clearly as she could his arms around her. As long as she was here, she might as well do some good.

Her ability to focus on and discern one creature at a time was a necessity in the populous sea, and Lyria called on it now to keep her awareness on Drew as he moved about the building from club to restaurant to kitchen. With each place he went, his level of frustration and displeasure rose. Part of it was his desire to come back to her, which was clear when he was called away, but as other things took his attention, other emotions were mixed in. By the time she saw him go into his office, he'd reached a near-boiling point of irritation. Either that or he really hated the door.

She smiled to herself as she finished the last sip of her margarita. She could think of a few wonderful ways to distract him they would both enjoy.

Lyria knew what humans thought of mermaids. It was clear from some of the erotic pictures they created and the stories they told. The name of the bar was even a hint at their beliefs. The truth was, mermaids and mermen weren't entirely promiscuous, but spending as much time as they did without clothes—whether in fin or leg form—they were not self-conscious about their bodies, nor did they see a reason not to enjoy themselves when another was willing.

Something about Drew excited her and she was

certain he was willing—or he would be. As soon as she could get his mind off of whatever was troubling him for the moment.

She knocked and heard his exasperated, "Oh God, what now?" before he called, "Come in."

He didn't look up when she walked in. "If you have another problem for me to solve, I'm done for the night. If the building's not on fire, it can wait until tomorrow."

"The building is fine, but I don't think we need to wait." The startled look on his face settled quickly into a smile, and Lyria knew interrupting him was the right decision. "I get the feeling when you are findable out there something always needs your attention, so I thought I might join you in here for a different kind of attention."

She walked behind his desk, stood in front of him, and bent down to kiss him. After his initial surprise, his mouth was warm and yielding and tasted of the drink she saw on his desk. He stood and put his arms around her, bringing her close to his body. Putting her hands on his shoulders, she enjoyed the play of muscles she'd felt on the dance floor and couldn't wait to feel his naked skin against hers.

"I'm dreaming," he said as they walked and kissed their way to the couch.

"Do you wish to be?"

"Good God, no. This is the best reality I've had in months."

She could sense the truth of his words and it made her heart sad for him. She wished she could soothe the worry and concern lurking beneath the surface. For now she brushed the awareness of his pain

44

aside, refocusing on the physical pleasure he was bringing her and which she could offer him. Tonight, enjoying his body and allowing him to please her was a much better use of her energy.

She broke the kiss to take his hand and walk them to the couch that was so conveniently in his office. Straddling his lap as he sat down, she undid the three buttons of his shirt, then found the bottom of it at his waist and pulled it up over his head. She was right about his build, muscled like a swimmer. She ran her hand down his chest, enjoying the feel of the coarse hair that lightly covered him, so different from the smooth skin and fine hair of mermen.

He dropped the straps of her dress off her shoulders, and with a gentle wiggle, it shimmied down to her waist. "I don't know how you did that, but I love it," he said as he caressed her breasts for the first time. She arched slightly, making certain to show him he pleased her and she wanted more. His hands appeared large on her frame, even though her breasts weren't small.

When he bent his head to kiss and suck her nipples, she worked to undo the belt and clasp of his pants. They had to separate and stand for her to take them off along with his underwear. It gave her the opportunity to caress his ass as she did so. Finding additional muscles heightened her pleasure. He was so wonderfully built.

"I realize we're already naked, and I'm not complaining," he said as he kicked his pants and shoes off, "but are you certain about this?"

Lyria smiled. Humans could get so concerned about emotions and sex, tying them together when it wasn't necessary. She also knew fewer males concerned themselves about this than did females and thought it spoke to his character that he stopped to ask. She liked when she was right about someone.

Kissing him deeply before she answered, she said, "Completely. Although I thought I made my desire fairly clear on the dance floor."

"You did, but I'm not used to a woman being so clear so quickly."

"I'm not like other women."

"No arguments here," he said as she pulled his mouth to her for another kiss.

Oh yes, she thought, she was going to enjoy her time with this one.

* * *

Even as he slid her dress off and he had visual confirmation she wore no underwear, Drew waited for her to come to her senses and stop him. When she did nothing other than continue to touch him, he relaxed, pulled her back onto the couch and enjoyed her effortless sexuality.

She took his breath away. Naked except for an unusual bracelet of charms and jewels, she was stunning. Creamy skin made her captivating green eyes stand out. Her lips were full, more so now from their kissing. Her hair flowed over the couch pillow in waves of red gold he couldn't help but touch. As tempting as it was, her body was even more so. He hardly knew where to start.

She dipped and curved in all the right places. Her breasts were full and lush, begging to be fondled and licked, which he did with great pleasure, enjoying how cool and smooth her skin was. Her scent made him think of sun and the smell of the beach at sunrise. Her waist was small, but her hips were rounded—more feminine then fashionable, which he preferred. He ran his hand over her gently rounded stomach, loving how she wasn't self-conscious about this part of her as so many women were, and then traced a red scar cutting from her hip inward.

"What happened here?'

She tensed for a moment then said, "Oh, I tangled with a Sea Dragon. They can get so nasty when they don't get what they want."

He smiled. "Yeah, I have a few wounds from stupid decisions, too."

Before he could ask her about the truth of the cut, she kissed him and clear thoughts when out of his head.

He couldn't get over her beauty. There was something so compelling and almost otherworldly about her. And she seemed to glow. Her hair caught the light from the desk and her skin was so soft and pale, it was as if she shimmered before him. Part of him expected that if he didn't keep his eyes on her she would disappear like an apparition created by his overworked brain.

But when her hands wrapped around his hard shaft and she fondled him gently, he was certain this was no dream and she wasn't going anywhere.

"You are so lovely," he said, moving back to her lips and kissing her again.

"Thank you," she said. He sighed with pleasure as she accepted his compliment without offering codicils or deflection. Already she was one of the most uncomplicated women he'd ever met. For the first time in months, he was glad to be where he was.

Then she ran her hands through his hair, down his back and toward his ass and he thought he could happily stay in his office forever.

She moved above him and continued to stroke his cock, making him harder and ready for her. Wanting to know if she was experiencing the same desire, he caressed her stomach and reached for her pussy. As he teased the flesh of her mound, he enjoyed the smooth hairless skin as well as her sigh, which told him of her pleasure as much as the way her legs gently opened for him.

He stroked the outer lips of her pussy, then pulled them apart so he could touch her intimately. With her moan came a wetness which made her as ready as he was. Feeling her response increased his excitement. As he slipped a finger inside, her muscles contracted around him, and it was his turn to moan. He leaned back to be able to see her better. At his new angle he could see her swollen pussy lips, her engorged clitoris peeking out from its hood. She was wonderfully responsive, natural and uncalculated. It was a huge change from the city women he'd been with most recently.

When he couldn't stand it any longer, he reached for his pants and pulled a condom out of his wallet. He thought he saw her wince as she moved, but the moment the condom was in place, she slid down on him, sheathing him within her in one movement.

He cried out, then bit it back before remembering the noise outside the room would cover any noise within. Lyria arched her back and placed her hands on his shoulders, which put her breasts in the perfect location for him to take them in his mouth again. He sucked hard on her nipples, enjoying the sounds she made as he excited her, thrilling to the feel of her getting wetter each time he pressed into her. When she threw back her head, her long hair brushed his legs. She, in turn, ran her hands everywhere she could, over his arms, his chest, even putting them behind her to grab his thighs. Her constant touches created a connection between them he didn't expect from a first encounter.

With his feet on the floor and her knees on the couch they were able to move together easily, and as his peak approached he reached for and gently rubbed at her clit, which swelled under his touch.

A thin sheen of sweat made her skin glisten. "Yes, please, yes," she said.

"God, yes, you feel so good."

"As do you. Please, don't stop because I'm going to…"

She rode him hard, grinding her hips into him as her climax hit. He was so caught up in watching her pleasure, his orgasm was delayed until she kissed him and brought him back to the moment. Then it hit like a dam bursting, weeks of being alone and detached disappearing under the need to be as close to her as possible. As he started to call out, she covered his mouth with hers, taking his release into her in every way.

When it was over he fell back against the couch, keeping his arms around her. She leaned her head against his shoulder as their breathing slowly returned to normal. After a minute, he brought her legs over to one side and lay back on the couch with her on top of him. He didn't know what to say and was grateful she was comfortable with the silence.

Unfortunately, it didn't last long and was broken by a knock at the door.

"Is the place on fire?" he called. He smiled when Lyria laughed, and he remembered he said the same to her when she arrived.

"No, boss, but we need you anyway. I tried to find you a few minutes ago and there was no answer when I knocked. There's a problem at the bar." The doorknob rattled and he gave Lyria a knowing look.

"You locked the door," he whispered.

"It seemed prudent, given how often we'd already been interrupted."

"You're amazing." He called, "I'll be out in a minute." He kissed Lyria and said quietly, "Even though I'd rather stay with you."

"I understand the importance of responsibilities. They can be maddening when they take you from what you desire."

"That's an understatement."

"But it doesn't change the situation."

"No, unfortunately not," he said.

She kissed him deeply, then let go so he could stand and find his clothes. Before his pants were zipped, she'd put her dress on and he found it excited him to watch it fall over her body. Especially knowing what was—and wasn't—underneath.

"I will try my best to make this quick," he said. "You can stay in here. There are drinks in the fridge."

She smiled. "You want me to stay?"

He kissed her. "Very much."

"You are sweet."

"It has nothing to do with being sweet. You're incredible."

"Take care of your business, Drew," she said and gave him a lingering kiss.

"You're not giving me a lot of incentive to leave."

"Knowing there will soon be another knock will have to be reason enough."

"Sadly, yes. I promise to be back as fast as I can." He gave her another kiss and left.

Ten minutes later an icy feeling rushed through Drew as he realized Lyria never agreed to be there when he returned. "I'll be right back," he told his bartender as they poured a drunk into a cab.

Part of him knew before he walked into his office what he would find, but he was still sorry when he discovered the room empty. He searched the top of his desk, then around the room looking for a phone number or a note, but there was no trace of Lyria.

Chapter Three

Lyria knew Drew wouldn't be pleased when he discovered she'd left, but between not knowing how long he'd be and knowing she'd be inviting trouble if she stayed, she decided it was best to slip out when he was distracted. Taking chances could be fatal, and not only for her.

As she walked back to her motel room, she thought she noticed a change in the air. Rain was coming. She breathed in deeply and winced. The pain was back. She put her hand on her hip and felt the soreness beneath the skin. Having sex, especially on top, might not have been the best choice given her injury, but the pleasure was greater than the pain and those moments with Drew were worth it.

To be honest, in the moment she forgot everything but how good Drew felt. While in his arms, Lyria forgot everything—her exile, the Sea Dragon, the weight of her responsibilities. She was glad to know his name in addition to how his kisses felt. He was strong and passionate and as soon as he was certain she wouldn't have second thoughts, gave himself over completely to their enjoyment. She liked the sandy color of his hair and the storm gray of his eyes, but mostly she liked bringing out the banked fire she sensed in him. He was not having a lot of fun in his life and she was glad to offer this to him.

She walked back to her motel along the mostly deserted boardwalk. She assumed most people had headed home to bed since tomorrow was a work day. She breathed in the scent of the ocean and let the sound of the waves calm her.

Which is why she was unprepared when her hand was grabbed and her arm nearly yanked out of its socket.

"Give us the bracelet and you won't get hurt, lady."

Lyria didn't recognize the voice but the word 'us' alerted her to there being more than one attacker. She reached out and sensed the filthy man from the store where she'd gotten the cash this morning. She wasn't surprised. She should have been more careful.

"I told you then but I'm willing to repeat myself. The bracelet is not available."

"Then we'll just have to take it from you."

A knife's cold point was pressed against her neck. She wasn't planning to struggle, but the blade enforced the decision. Her assailant nicked her skin to show he wasn't joking.

"Now, once again, missy. Give us the bracelet."

She said nothing, not really knowing what she could do. She had no weapons and the two men were certainly larger and stronger than she was. *Melusine, guide me. Help me.*

As she thought the last two words there was a warming sensation that started at the center of the bracelet and was followed by a feeling of electricity that started at her wrist then coursed through her body.

"Dude, look at the diamond."

Sapphire, you fool, she thought, not that it mattered. She looked down and saw what the man did. The bracelet was glowing.

A moment later it emitted a bright flash of light as well as a pulse that threw the men away from her and left her free to run. She took a moment to sense that they were still alive. They were, but unconscious. Good. That would allow her to get away without them seeing where she was going.

She took off her shoes, and, carrying them, she ran the rest of the way to her motel, slipping inside her room as quickly as possible. She stood against the door breathless and still somewhat frightened.

The bracelet had never responded like that. She'd called on its strength and power on several occasions when she was needed to heal, but tonight, the magic protected her. That was a first. She was unnerved, but grateful.

Very grateful.

When her heart beat settled, she took off the rest of her clothes and checked her injuries in the mirror. The cut from the knife was easily healed. She had felt the gash created by Fiero pull when her attackers grabbed her, and as she placed healing scales over it, she did what she could to imbue them with some of the newly awakened magic from the Stone.

The bracelet could protect her as well as heal others. She couldn't get over it. There was so much more to the Stone of Clarity than she knew. Perhaps this would keep her and the Stone safe if Fiero found her and attempted to separate them. The power of the stone would be deadly in the wrong hands. There was no telling what Fiero planned for the Stones if he reunited them or what could happen if it was under his control. She must remain safe, because if something happened to her there would be no one to stop him.

She needed water. Warm water surrounding her body, offering her body and her mind some relief. She ran herself a hot bath. It wasn't as nice as a natural hot spring or even the large tub she had in her home, but it would be enough for tonight.

The heat felt wonderful on her skin and soothed muscles that were tight from worry. And a little sore from sex.

Lyria smiled and let the warmth sink in.

After magically drying herself, she got under the covers and forced her thoughts away from the muggers, the bracelet and Fiero to more pleasant images.

Drew would be lovely company as she passed her enforced time on land, much more exciting than she expected. When she saw him at The Siren her initial intention was only to flirt, but when he joined her on the dance floor and he was close, things changed. Rapidly. She was drawn to him, to the pain and loneliness she sensed—so different from the strength and hope of the man who saved the drowning girl all those years ago. Recognizing his vulnerabilities were similar to hers, Lyria knew she must be careful to keep things physical, not emotional, between them.

He was certainly sexy enough to make it possible, but as she climbed into bed she reminded herself she couldn't take chances. The sheets weren't as soft as her own bedding, but knowing she couldn't be found helped her relax enough to fall asleep.

That, and thoughts of Drew naked.

* * *

She was out there, the slippery creature, and no matter what or how long it took, he was going to find her and claim her—along with the precious piece of Melusine's band. The three bracelets together were necessary to his plan. He needed the Stone of Clarity, but somehow he sensed it was further than it had ever been, and that knowledge made him furious.

Shifting his body from dragon to human form, Fiero stomped through his lair, an intricate series of caves beneath his island home, which belonged to him alone since the death of his father. It was large enough to accommodate him in his dragon mode, but he burned more energy and had more room to pace this way. Fury in his dragon form tended to cause damage, both intentional and unintentional. He did not want additional concerns at this time.

"How may I assist you?" came an expected but unannounced request. His family had always kept naiads in their service. For generations these smaller shifters faithfully served sea dragons, although whether out of fear or loyalty it was never clear. Nor did it matter.

"I wish to be left alone," Fiero yelled. It was a good thing he was in his human guise. Telepathic communication in dragon form was possible, but when he was this angry he tended to knock lesser minds into unconsciousness with his temper.

"As you say, my lord. A meal has been left out in the dining area. Please let me know if there is anything else you require." The naiad disappeared as quietly as he had entered.

Fiero didn't want to eat. He wanted to rage and shake the walls until the inlaid jewels shook free. Nothing could ease him until the Stone of Clarity was his.

He should have possessed the stone long ago, and it was driving him insane knowing the power of it lay with a merfamily which, by right and contract, should be connected to him.

The first time he approached Lyria, he tried seduction. The attention he received when he was in his legged form told him he was attractive, and he hoped to be able to create a bond with her this way. Her willingness would not only have made things easier, but would have freed up the magic of the stone.

And she was appealing. Pretty he supposed, although he preferred his women with dark hair and eyes. It wouldn't be a hardship to have her as a mate.

When she didn't respond to him, he added magic. His kind had strong powers of persuasion that worked hypnotically on lower beings, such as the naiads. But the wench was not deceived. It was as if the Stone kept her clear-headed and he was unable to sway her. In fact, it was as if the more he lied or tried to compel her, the more she heard the truth.

"The Stone and I will never belong to you," she said.

He was surprised by her sudden outburst. "I did not ask."

"You didn't have to. It is clear you have no interest in me. I can sense your desires and your hunger for power. You will not claim the Stone of Clarity or the other stones, and you will most certainly not have me."

"You cannot keep me from what I want," he said as his lower half transformed from human legs to tail. He reached for her with the scaled appendage, but she dove into the water, shifting her own body as she did so. When she surfaced a distance away, she said to him, "I will never be caught nor contained by the likes of you."

But she would. He would see to it. He would show his father how wrong he'd been about his younger son. Even if the old man was dead, Fiero could still prove himself the rightful leader of the Kelpies and Sea Dragons.

He was not his father's intended heir. That honor was bestowed on his brother, Yacopo, older by eight years, and a pure blooded Kelpie. Fiero did not even know he had a brother until he was ten years old and his mother lay dying. They had lived a mostly isolated life. She explained to him that although she was a mermaid, he was the product of two Oceanides, and she did not know where he would fit in. She hoped he would find his place, but she couldn't tell him much about his father's side. She answered his questions about merfolk, but always with a combination of bitterness and sadness for the way they treated her when she was pregnant.

On the day she lay dying, his absent father came to claim him. Fiero didn't want to go, but when his mother insisted, he stopped his restless shifting from one form to another. His father was pleased with his strength and outward dragon appearance, but once they were back in his home, it was clear Fiero was the inferior child, and Yacopo the favored.

Not that the two boys cared. They were instantly

delighted in each other and became inseparable for the next several years. Only when Yacopo needed to take his private lessons with their father were they apart. At those times, Fiero practiced his fighting skills so that when his brother became their leader, he could stand proudly at his side. As long as he had his brother, the fact their father rarely took notice of him didn't matter. He was used to being alone. Yacopo was enough.

The two were adventurous and curious, causing frequent havoc in their home which horrified most of the inhabitants, but delighted their father. One day however, shortly after Fiero's 15th birthday, they ventured too far and deep and unintentionally entered the lair of the Leviathan, distant relations of the Kelpie and their kin who guarded the Underworld. When they realized what they had done, they tried to escape undetected, but it was impossible. A whirlpool came up to claim them, inside of which were the sharpened bones and scales of the Leviathan's previous prey. Both of them were cut and scraped, but kept swimming until they were back in their own territory.

It was then Fiero saw how badly Yacopo had been injured. While Fiero received gashes and several nearly bone deep cuts, Yacopo's skin was significantly pierced by several pieces of bone. Healers were called, but nothing could be done. Yacopo died two days later. The world of land suffered for weeks as Fiero's father churned the waters in his grief.

Fiero became his father's heir, but there was no joy in the title for either of them. On several occasions Fiero was told he should have died, and the young dragon agreed. His father stayed away from him as much as possible and Fiero was left to educate and raise himself. He was helped by the arrival of his father's brother, Balban. His uncle, not having a previous bias and knowing that Fiero would lead one day, did what he could to provide guidance. He was also the one to show Fiero the contract from Lyria's father.

The contract gave him new hope, but not much more. There was no fun, no joy, no laughter or love. Life was bleak without his brother.

Fifteen years had passed since Yacopo's death and with his father gone as well, it was time for Fiero to have the control and power he desired. The Stones and the little healer would ensure this for him.

It didn't matter how far Lyria swam or where she hid. He would claim what he wanted and he did not care what he had to do to accomplish this. If he was to be feared and shunned, then he was going to give the seas and all those who dwelled in it a damn good reason to fear him and teach a lesson to those who turned their backs on him.

* * *

Her knees buckled. Rare for a mermaid.

One of the stones, and probably the mermaid who wore it, was threatened. She didn't know if it was the Stone of Clarity or of Strength. It couldn't be the Stone of Love, that was safely—if unfortunately—with her. Her heart was racing, probably in time with the mermaid being attacked. She hoped for the mermaid's safety, feeling helpless and hating the emotion.

Should she try and discover if it was Lyria or Amina who was in jeopardy? Could she help even if she knew? She had an idea where they were. It made it easier for her to remain apart from them. No, she would continue to keep her distance and her secret. To them the Stone of Love was missing.

And she intended to keep it that way.

* * *

As Lyria had anticipated, the next morning dawned gray and drizzly. She put on another dress and headed out to the beach early. There were no lifesaving people out and she walked out as far as she could on the rocks. She looked for signs of anyone watching her and when she found none, she slipped out of the dress, put it and the shoes in her bag, and dove, finning—shifting her legs to fins—before she touched the water.

After swimming south for an hour, she sent a short call, almost like a telepathic whistle, to Amina. She waited, then swam on for another 30 minutes and repeated the process. This time she received three short whistles back, which was all the information she needed. For the next three hours Lyria swam at a speed humans would find impossible and arrived at an underwater building she hadn't visited in years.

You had to pick the family burial site? she asked her cousin telepathically. Because it was necessary to communicate through the murkiness and silence of water, merfolk developed additional means of interaction.

Amina shrugged. *It was the safest place I could think of on short notice as well as given how far north your call came from. You've gone back to—*

Don't think it, Lyria said. *Safe or not, we have to*

61

be especially careful. Fiero's power and control have clearly grown and we do not know everyone who is under his influence, or where they are.

You're right, of course, but all the more reason for you to choose a location you have never visited.

No one but you knows of my trips there, Amina. Who would believe it, anyway?

Amina's expression showed the same thing as her words: She didn't agree with Lyria's choice. One of the few things Lyria liked about being on land was that no one could read her as quickly as other merfolk did. It would be a relief, as well as an advantage she would have over humans.

You should not be taking chances, Lyria. Last night I thought I sensed you. Not your thoughts, something else. What were you doing?

What she was doing was having sex with a hot human. She was not sharing that with Amina at this point and she kept the focus on the concerns about Fiero.

I assure you, I'm not taking chances. I am surrounded and masked by humans in an area nowhere near where I am usually seen by merfolk. There is no community within 200 miles.

Amina must have decided Lyria couldn't be swayed because she changed the subject. *I heard good news from the Pacific. Your* rusalka, *Emma, is well and adjusting beautifully to her life with her new family. She's happy and healthy. You made a good choice.*

Lyria smiled as she thought about the beautiful girl who six months ago was thrown half dead into the sea by her uncaring foster parents. Emma was still alive when she hit the waters off the coast of Georgia and her dying life force sent out a call through the ocean. The Stone of Clarity had warmed against Lyria's skin and her entire body came alive. She was immediately transported to where the girl was being pulled out by the tides.

Melusine's Band not only made the wearer the people's healer but with the Stone it also granted the gift of regeneration. Should someone die suddenly, either because of or near the water, and their spirit reached out for help, Lyria was drawn to them and given the opportunity to offer assistance. It didn't happen often, and it unnerved her each time she was called upon to make the decision.

With Emma, it was an easy decision. The child was precious and innocent with a fierce will to live. Lyria knew the moment she touched her that the merfolk would be blessed to have her as one of them. Before others could arrive to assist, Emma's transformation to a merchild was complete. She was given into the care of a couple who had no children of their own, and it was wonderful to learn she was doing well.

It was a gift not to be used casually. Not everyone whom the sea claimed could or should be allowed to live on. A mistake not only harmed the new merfolk, but often the community as a whole. It was her greatest and most overwhelming ability.

She feared this power was what the Sea Dragon truly coveted. She couldn't imagine he cared about her capacity to heal, unless he was injured. If Lyria was under his influence, so was the control over who lived and who died. Power could not be placed in the wrong hands.

Focusing again on her cousin, she thought, *Thank you for telling me. I needed to hear something positive. Is there any other news?*

Naiads were seen immediately after you left, in the area around the fight with you and Fiero. No one could tell what they were doing precisely, although it appeared as though they were collecting something.

That can't be good. It was not necessary even to wonder about it. Nothing the Sea Dragon did was good for her. *No word as to how he intends to find me or what precisely he has planned for the Stone of Clarity?*

Amina shook her head and her red gold plaits danced behind her. The graceful movement was in direct opposition to the worry on her features. Lyria reached out and took her cousin's hand. *It will work out. Worry not, my* haratrela, Lyria said, using an endearment meaning "one who brings me joy and drives me crazy."

I will always worry for you, Lyria, as will Uncle Costin and all those who love and care for you. You are our healer, yes, but so very much more. You are always my cousin and friend first. Please, don't ever forget. I am as worried about you being with the Sea Dragon as I am for the Stone of Clarity.

Lyria would have liked to brush aside the comments but since merfolk were also able to sense strong emotions, she had no doubt that Amina was telling the truth. It moved her greatly and, not having words, she opened her arms to embrace her cousin. Amina swam up and into the hug and put Lyria's head on her shoulder.

You have so much strength in you, more than you can even imagine, Amina said. Lyria felt as though she were the younger one, but didn't try to correct or interrupt her cousin. For the moment she needed comforting, something she didn't normally accept. She could allow herself to let down her guard with Amina, if nowhere else.

It's a three-hour swim back, Lyria said, finally letting go. *Is there anything else I need to know?*

There is one other thing. Did something happen last night?

Lyria wondered if she could blush underwater. And what made Amina ask the question I the first place. *Well, there was a human male…*

Amina put a hand. *Stop. No. That's not it.*

Lyria thought for a moment. *Oh, I was attacked.*

'Oh, I was attacked'? How were you found? Are you okay? What happened?

Not by an Oceanide, Lyria assured her. *Humans. Thieves. They saw the bracelet and tried to steal it.*

How did you get away?

The bracelet protected me.

It what? Amina's expression was so shocked it was almost amusing. Lyria told her what happened, explaining how power from the bracelet enabled her to escape.

Your fear must have been strong and I sensed that. Be careful, Lyria. You and I are connected so that's why I felt it, but I don't want you found.

Thank you. I will be careful. Promise. Anything else?

Lyria could see Amina thinking before answering, *I think that's everything I won't contact you unless it's an emergency. I hope not to have to see you until we've passed the third day after the full moon.*

I hope the same. Be well.
And you, Lyria. And you.

Lyria arrived back in Point Pleasant as the evening lights on the boardwalk were starting to come on. The place appeared to glitter. Families were slowly being replaced by couples holding hands. The tinny sounds of the arcades were being overpowered by music coming from the clubs. She picked up a few necessities at a small store and passed by The Siren on her way to her motel. Tonight a board out front advertised an '80s music night. She didn't know what this meant, but from the early crowd she assumed it must be a good thing.

When she arrived in her room she immediately kicked off her shoes. No matter the style, she hated them. Of all the things humans wore, it was her least favorite of the unavoidable choices. She would have to take time to walk on the sand while she was here to get some relief.

She also wanted to spend time with Drew. At first, she considered not going back and possibly going to another club so as not to be predictable to anyone who could be watching, but she knew in her heart she wanted to see him again. There was so little about the overall situation she liked, she decided she was going to at least enjoy who she would spend it with.

And she'd enjoyed Drew quite a bit the night before.

He not only excited her, but she felt safe with him as well. In fact, after last night, she'd ask him to walk her home tonight to make certain she wasn't attacked again.

As she brushed her hair out of its braid and put it up in combs, she thought about their dance and the hot but hurried sex in his office. Perhaps there would be time tonight for something a little longer. Her body tingled at the thought. He really was incredibly sexy and it would be more than a little pleasurable to take her time with him.

She finished dressing, putting back on the dreaded shoes, and headed out.

The crowd at The Siren had grown, but the guard from the night before recognized her and let her in. She walked through the crowds, taking in the carefree spirit she sensed from the people.

"Hey, it's the margarita lady," called the bartender.

"Yes, how did you remember with so many people?"

"Because I have never seen anyone enjoy a drink the way you did last night. Can I get you another tonight? Maybe one with strawberry in it?"

"Will it still have the sour taste? That was my favorite part, next to the salt."

"Absolutely."

"Then I'd love one."

As she waited for her drink, a single seat opened at the bar and she slid into it, grateful to have a little personal space among all the pushing patrons.

"Ah, there you are," the bartender said as he brought her a light red drink with the requisite salted rim. "Thought I'd lost you for a moment."

"Not a chance." She took a sip and sighed. "Oh, that is very, very good. Thank you."

"Joe. And you're welcome."

"I'm Lyria." She held out her hand and he shook it.

"Good to officially meet you." He picked up a

glass and toasted her with it. "Don't remember seeing you around before last night."

"I only arrived yesterday."

"Are you staying long?"

"Sadly, no, I'll be gone three days after the full moon."

"Excuse me?"

Lyria shook her head as if to clear it. She forgot humans didn't track the days the same as they did in the sea. She did a mental recalculation before saying, "I'm here until Tuesday."

"Well, not a long visit, but I'm sure you'll have fun. There's plenty to enjoy while you're here."

"There certainly is." And for tonight, she knew exactly where she wanted to start. As he spoke, Lyria spotted Drew on the other side of the dance floor, talking with a server, then heading to the kitchen. She tried to sense the mood he was in, but there were too many people around and the moment she opened her senses, she was flooded with thoughts and images, mostly dealing with sex of one sort or another. She took a long drink of her margarita to cool her down.

"Ouch," she wailed and put her hand to her forehead.

Joe was there in a moment. "What's wrong?"

"I don't know. My head feels like it might explode."

"Brain freeze."

"What?" It sounded alarming.

Her dread must have shown on her face because Joe laughed and said, "First experience with that, too, I gather. It's what happens when you drink something very cold, very fast. Here, a glass of water will help. Just take a sip."

She did and the pain started to ease. "Oh, thank you. Much better."

"What's much better?"

Lyria jumped and turned to see Drew looking at her with concern and curiosity. "My head."

"What did Joe do to your head?"

"Nothing, Drew," they said at the same time. Lyria put her hand on his arm. "I was drinking too fast and because it's cold, or so Joe tells me, my brain froze."

Drew laughed. "Okay, that's a unique way to put it. Glad you're fine."

"I am, thank you."

"Well enough to dance?"

"Are you asking?"

He held out a hand and she joined him. The music was loud, the beat easy to find. After a few minutes she asked, "What's a comma chameleon?"

He leaned toward her ear and said, "Karma Chameleon."

She nodded then shook her head. "Nope, I still don't understand what it is."

"No one does. Welcome to the hits of the 1980s, when MTV made stars out of the most unlikely performers. I'd just go with it."

And she did. The words might have made no sense, but the dancing was fun and it was easy to pick up on the energy of the crowd and enjoy the freedom. She spun, clapped, and let Drew twirl and dip her on occasion. Dancing was one of those things she loved about being on land. It was not quite the same in water, and although merfolk created beautiful music of their own, it wasn't even close to this.

Two songs later the beat slowed down and the floor cleared of the singles. When Drew held out a hand, Lyria took it and was pulled into his arms.

"Nice to have you back," he said

"It's nice to be back."

"Then why did you disappear after last night?"

She was expecting the question, but she foolishly hadn't prepared an answer. "I wasn't certain about staying. I got a little carried away last night."

"We both did. Were you sorry?"

"Not at all. I'm the one who sought you out, remember?"

"Vividly. So why didn't you stay?"

She put her head on his shoulder and didn't say anything, simply allowed the music to carry her for a bit as she thought of one of the lyrics she heard. *You're so close but still a world away.* The sentiment was very accurate. She felt a connection to him, yet knew it was only temporary. Their time together had a built-in end and whether she wanted to think about it or not. Five days was all she had. They had.

Moving her head, she kissed him and said, "I thought leaving was the smarter decision. Sometimes people say things they don't mean in the heat of the moment. I didn't want you to come back and realize you made a mistake."

"And why did you come back tonight?"

"In case you decided you didn't."

He smiled. "You are definitely not a mistake."

"What a lovely thing to hear."

"Tell me you won't disappear again tonight."

"The night is still young. You might change your mind," she said.

"I won't."

"Confident, aren't you?"

"Absolutely. I know what I want and what I want is you."

"That sounds wonderful, but can we keep dancing for now?"

He laughed. "Of course."

"Thank you, it's been too long since I last danced."

He gave her a squeeze and a soft kiss. "No problem. By the way, don't think I didn't notice you're not wearing a bra again."

"You'll never catch me wearing one. I hate the things. Underwear, too. They always feel as though they're limiting my movements." She knew Oceanides who liked the lacy underthings. Amina had quite a collection, although no matter what humans thought, no one would ever wear a shell bra. She laughed.

"What's funny?"

She had to come up with something. "I was thinking maybe you'd prefer I wore underwear. Do you mind that I don't?"

"Does the sun mind shining?"

"Not as far as I know."

"Then you have your answer," he said.

When the song ended and the next one was fast, Drew gestured toward the bar where Joe had her seat and a drink for Drew waiting.

"What concoction did he make for you?" she asked as she watched him take a healthy swallow.

"Something very exotic. Club soda and lime. Too many things demand my attention for me to be able to drink alcohol during business hours. However, just before he closes up for the night, Joe will pour me a Drambuie on ice, which will help wash away the strains and stress of the evening. Unless, of course," he said, moving close to her ear and licking the inside, making her shiver, "you want something different."

"I don't know. I've never had Drambuie. It could be better."

He laughed. "I never know what response I'm going to get from you. You go from sweet to sassy so quickly."

"And you like that."

"Yes, as a matter of fact, I do."

* * *

She was completely open and a total mystery, Drew thought, and he loved the puzzle of it. Which surprised him. He'd had too many mysteries, to many unknowns which had come back to bite him in the ass and for the last few months he preferred the known and uncomplicated. Lyria seemed to be anything but that.

Of course, no woman could be known in a day, but already she was a bundle of exciting contradictions and he wanted to know more. She sought him out for sex but disappeared when given the opportunity to stay. She offered kisses and touches freely, and yet he sensed something aloof and removed in her. She oozed sex appeal while being cool and detached from the reactions of others. Seriously, there was hardly a man in the room who didn't notice her. Hell, a lot of the women had, most with envy and annoyance.

But most importantly she'd returned and tonight

he was going to make certain she didn't disappear so quickly again. He was about to ask her what had brought her to Point Pleasant when they were interrupted, no surprise, by something needing his attention.

"I plan to come back when I can, but I can't say when that will be."

"I know," she said. "We did this dance yesterday."

"I want you to be here when I'm done for the evening."

She smiled. "I know."

"Good, as long as I'm clear this time. Joe, if she tries to leave, use duct tape to keep her still."

"Yes, boss," he said with a salute.

He took her hand and gave it a kiss before taking a sip of his drink and heading to his office to deal with a crying server. Sometimes the minutia of the business drove him insane, but it had to be done if Mr. V. was going to be able to take things back over in a few months and so Drew could return to his life.

And what life would that be, a voice said in his head. His old business was unsalvageable, and he had no clear idea what he was going to do next. Skills and experience he had. A plan—not so much.

Suddenly the distractions of the club were a welcome relief. He wasn't ready to think about what he was going to do after he was done here. He calmed down the frustrated server and threw out the patrons who had been harassing her. Drunk or sober, he wouldn't accept clients who didn't know how to treat women properly.

He stepped back into the club and looked around to see if he could spot his next crisis. Out of the corner of his eye he saw Lyria and let her be a distraction. As she crossed her legs, her purple dress fluttered and opened along a slit. She had gorgeous long legs, and he liked the way the color set off her beautiful pale skin.

Soft skin.

Which heated when he kissed and stroked her.

Ah, yes, a much better distraction.

Truthfully, she'd been on his mind all day and it was a relief when he saw her at the bar. He had a moment of jealousy when he noticed her smiling at Joe, which was foolish since his bartender was gay and, according to rumors, in a committed relationship for the last several years. Still, her appeal was so obvious to Drew, he couldn't help but think she would be attracting a great deal of attention if he didn't make it clear to other men she was with him.

When Drew finally made it back to the bar, Lyria was talking with the woman next to her and looking horrified.

"Tell me again what are they called?" Lyria said.

"Fishnet stockings. You've never heard of them?"

"I've heard of fishnets, of course, something that captures the fish and brings them to their death in large numbers."

The woman laughed. "Well, yes, but these get their name because the pattern resembles those nets. You don't use them for fishing. They're considered very sexy."

Lyria appeared doubtful.

"I wear them because I like the way they make my legs look," the woman added and she held her legs out so Lyria, and others, could admire them.

"So do I," said the man next to her, joining the

conversation and giving the woman a kiss. "Nothing fishlike about them."

Drew whispered in her ear, "I assume if you don't like underwear, you're not a fan of stockings either."

She turned and gave him a smile. "Not at the moment. I can't see why anyone would want to wear something meant to confine or capture fish."

"When you put it like that, I can see your point. When I can remember why I've found them sexy in the past, however, I'll point out to you the times when they are quite nice."

"If you insist, but I hope you won't mind if I skip wearing them."

He thought about all luscious skin which at the moment was only one thin layer of fabric away from him. "I don't mind in the least."

They kissed and he ran his hand down her back to prove his words. When she shivered with pleasure, his cock started to harden. Her easy responses drove him mad—in a good way. He had women attracted to him, but there was something so honest about her reactions it set his blood racing. He ached to leave with her immediately, but it was too early, and Thursdays were generally busy.

"Do you have anyplace else to be for the evening?" he asked.

"No, I have nothing planned while I'm here."

The teenage boy who lived forever in every man's head gave a cheer. "Then will you stay here and wait for me to be done for the night?"

She kissed him again and said, "I will."

"I'll send you some food to absorb the tequila in your margarita."

75

"That sounds lovely."

The night crawled by. It didn't matter how busy he was; every time he looked at the clock it had barely moved. Finally when it was only Joe and a few servers, he asked the bartender if he'd close up. Joe agreed with a knowing smile, and Drew took Lyria's hand and walked away from the bar. Once they were in the empty restaurant, he pulled her to him for a passionate kiss. He opened her mouth with his tongue, tasting her, needing her. "Come home with me." He couldn't tell if he meant it as a request or an order.

Not that it mattered. There was only one answer he wanted to hear.

"With pleasure," she replied.

That was the one.

Although she came to him easily the night before, he couldn't help but be surprised at how quickly she agreed to join him tonight. He'd become so jaded he took nothing for granted and still assumed anyone might suddenly change directions and intentions on him at any time.

He held his hand out and she gave him hers with no hesitation and with a smile on her face he wanted to see there all the time. There were no questions, no pretense of wanting anything other than the same thing he did. It made his desire grow, which he didn't think possible.

Chapter Four

For the first time since his return, Drew was glad to be living directly above the restaurant. He wondered what Lyria would think of it, but didn't know he was nervous until he breathed a sigh of relief when she proclaimed it lovely. She walked around, touching the shelves and furniture, pronouncing things warm and charming. He was aching for her to touch him the same way. Breathing in deeply, she said, "I love how you can smell the ocean in here. It's probably as close as one can get without actually living in it."

"I never noticed it before," he said, but her mentioning it did make him aware of it. Of course, she was making him aware of a lot of things, mostly his growing need to have her close to him.

It didn't take long before she walked back, put her arms around him and she kissed him deeply, finally pressing her body fully against his, which she hadn't done enough of when they had danced. Then all he could do was breathe in her scent, which resembled the ocean mixed with something floral and decidedly feminine. "You have a great mouth," she said when the kiss ended.

Without music and noise to distract him, he

noticed she had an unusual accent. Melodic and smooth but a touch foreign. "Where are you from? I can't place your accent."

"Over a thousand miles south of here." He pictured a map in his mind and figured it must be in or around Florida. "I speak a lot of different languages, which probably influences my speech. Are you truly interesting in talking?"

"Not in the least," he said and recaptured her mouth. She responded fully, sliding her tongue between his lips, swirling it gently in his mouth, making him think of what else she could do with it. She was intoxicating.

Her hands were on his chest and when she moved them, he wondered where she'd place them next. She surprised him when she took two steps back and untied the halter at the back of her neck, letting her dress fall in a pool of material at her feet. He couldn't get over her curves. Her breasts were lush and full and her hips rounded, her waist tiny in comparison. Her stomach wasn't flat, an aspect of her body that continued to delight him. It made her more real, and he adored that she didn't try to hide any part of herself. There wasn't an inch of her he didn't want to touch and taste. She kicked off the tiny sandals she wore and walked back into his arms.

Never before had a woman been naked for him so quickly. Or so naturally. Not including last night, he amended. If he thought her beautiful before, she took his breath away tonight with her confidence in her needs and passion. He ran his hand down her ass and cupped the soft tight globes in his hands as her breasts pressed against him. He found it wildly exciting to be with a woman who was so clearly comfortable with her own body.

When he finally broke the kiss to look into her eyes, take in the loveliness of her face, he traced her lips with his finger, marveling at their soft fullness. Her tongue peeked out and licked him briefly. There was more fire in that touch from her than in full orgasms from other women. He'd been with women who were sexy and appealing on the outside, but had nothing burning in them to give. Hell, he'd been with too many women who fit that description. Lyria was more refreshing than his evening swims. To have desire coupled with openness was indescribably wonderful.

"You are wearing too many clothes, Drew," she said as he continued to stare at her.

"I agree."

As he undid the remaining buttons of his polo shirt, Lyria reached directly for his pants. She quickly opened the button, unzipped the fly, and the weight of his wallet and phone in the pockets caused the pants to fall directly to the floor. Her hands stroked the edge of his boxers, a finger dipping below the elastic, touching the skin and making him gasp. He pulled his shirt over his head and her attention moved to his chest. She caressed the skin from his collarbone down, running fingers through his chest hair and following the line it made back to his shorts. Putting both hands on his hips, she tugged down on the material for it to join his chinos on the floor. He felt a little foolish standing naked in a pool of clothes so he quickly stepped out of them, kicking off his boat shoes in the process.

He wrapped his hands around her small waist and

pulled her close, feeling her naked skin against his. It was electric. Her skin was slightly cool and it only made him feel hotter.

She kissed him deeply. He couldn't wait to have her pressing against him.

"My bed. I need you in my bed."

"Lead the way," she said.

Instead of leading, he did something he'd never done. He put one hand around her waist and another behind her knees and scooped her up into his arms. He'd always thought it to be silly and cliché. Tonight, it was right.

He continued kissing her as he carried her across the living room to the bedroom. He placed her in the middle of the king size bed and turned a bedside lamp on low. He didn't want to miss anything with her, not how her skin glowed, or how her face flushed. Something about her made him bold and hungry—and he loved it.

He joined her on the cool sheets, as she reached behind her to pull out whatever was holding her long hair pinned up. When the last clip was removed, her red hair spilled everywhere, nearly covering her, until she tossed it behind her. He'd never seen hair as long or full and he expected it would be wonderful in his hands. However, for now all he wanted to feel was her body. It was clear she agreed with his idea since once her hands were free, she reached out and pulled him closer.

Nestled between her legs, he could feel the wetness of her pussy against his cock. Knowing she was as ready as he was caused him to surge further, and he couldn't recall if he'd ever been this hard for a woman before. "I want all of you," he said hoarsely.

"I can tell," she said. Wiggling her hips beneath him, he was treated to the heat spilling out of her. "I am aching too. I want to touch you and taste you. Say there will be time for everything."

"There will be, my beauty, if you want it as much as I do."

"I definitely do."

The night before was rushed and frantic and, as wonderful as it was, tonight Drew wanted to take his time. Seeing her laid out on his bed like a succulent meal prepared especially for him was the most enticing thing he'd ever experienced.

He started at her collarbone, tracing where it created a gentle hollow. He placed kisses at the base of her throat as she ran her fingers through his hair and across the back of his shoulders. When her heart rate jumped, he could feel it beneath his lips. His hands stroked the curves of her lush breasts, enjoying their weight and fullness in his hands. With the tip of his tongue, he teased a nipple and his excitement grew as it hardened under his attention. He took more of it into his mouth, sucking and swirling as he intended to do to another sensitive part of her body. He gently pinched the other nipple so the sensations would be balanced. Her soft sighs were wonderful, making him hope she would continue to be as responsive.

Tracing a line between her breasts with his tongue, his hands caressed her hips as he moved his body lower. Her skin was soft and cool beneath his touch and he loved the feel of the muscles in her thighs as they tensed, then relaxed. He was looking forward to feeling them wrapped around him, but first he wanted to stay focused on her pleasure.

He moved her legs open, waiting to see what her reaction would be. Not every woman he'd known liked the intimacy of oral sex and he wanted to give her an opportunity to refuse. He was thrilled when she moved them a little wider, giving him more access to her. Stroking the insides of her thighs, he teased his way up each side, moving deliberately, wanting to enjoy every inch of her

With one finger, he traced along the outside of her pussy, barely touching the lips. Since she was bare in the soft light of the room, it was easy to see them swell and his body hardened further in response. The lightest bit of moisture was already visible. He remembered how wet she became the night before and ached to make her feel that way again. From the moment she'd been in his arms on the dance floor this evening, he'd wanted her like this, naked and spread for him.

Kissing his way down her body, he licked at her creamy skin, enjoying her tiny shivers. Grateful for the king-sized mattress that gave him plenty of room, he moved so he was completely between her legs, then gave the slowest of licks over the softness, staying above the most sensitive parts with his mouth but teasing her gently with his finger.

She gripped the sheets as her body responded to the intimate caress. He breathed in the scent of her arousal and couldn't wait any longer to taste her. He moved lower and covered her pussy with his tongue, lapping her from top to bottom. Her taste was sweet and salty, intoxicating. As if she was made for him to enjoy.

"Drew, yes," she said and arched her back up, giving him better access to her core. He felt her pull at the sheets with pleasure.

Aching to give her more, he brushed his tongue tip over her clit, twirling it around the hardened bud. It swelled under his attention and he sucked it into his mouth, making her cry out again.

He wanted to make her speechless. As he continued to lick and tease her, he slid first one, then two fingers deep inside of her. Her body responded in a rush of wetness, which he eagerly lapped. Seeing her clitoris swell thrilled him. He couldn't remember being so hungry for a woman, wanting her to be as needy as he was and he wanted to please her beyond anything anyone had ever done for her in the past. Pumping his fingers, he bent them, increasing the sensations building inside of her. Every movement of his resulted in a response from her, whether a moan, an encouraging "yes," or her legs opening wider.

He looked up from her pussy and the image was one of the most erotic he had ever seen. Her legs were spread wide, her hair fanned out behind her, her breasts full, nipples hard. She was ready, available, and entirely his to enjoy.

Bringing his mouth back to her pussy, he was determined to give her pleasure the way she had for him the night before. Laving her entrance as he continued to thrust with his fingers, he felt her climax build. When she could barely get his name out and grabbed his hair with her hands, he knew she was close. He circled her clit with his tongue, then flicked it up and down as her climax neared.

Pressing up with his fingers and moving his tongue as quickly as he could, her orgasm rushed through her body. She wrapped her legs around him, holding him close as she yelled his name and called to a goddess he didn't recognize. She fed him her pussy, pressing it closer to him and he enjoyed every inch of her, taking all she offered him. He'd never seen a woman so beautiful or free with her responses.

It was madly exciting. He couldn't remember the last time he'd enjoyed giving a woman pleasure as much.

As her breathing began to return to normal, he gentled his movements and reveled in the shivers continuing to run through her. He slowly kissed his way up her body, licking and sucking first her stomach, then beneath her breasts, then finally her nipples. She kept her legs around him the entire time. There was no space between them.

By the time they were face to face, he was hungry for her lips and he captured them in a deep kiss, not caring if she minded the taste of herself on him.

As he caressed her hips, she slid a hand between them and wrapped it around his cock, stroking him slowly, pulling back the foreskin and exposing the sensitive head. He wondered for a brief moment if being uncut would bother her, but all she said was, "Please, be inside me."

Not seeing a reason to argue with a beautiful woman, he reached into his bedside table, took out a condom, there by habit not necessity until now, then ripped it open and slid it over his cock. For the second night in a row, he was amazed at the intensity between them. This was beyond feeling horny. He needed this woman.

She ran her nails over his back and placed kisses on his chest as she spoke "Show me you want this as much as I do. I want you as deep inside of me as possible."

He lifted her hips to him, placed the head of his cock against her entrance and thrust himself into her.

* * *

By the tides, he felt good. She opened herself wider to accommodate him and wrapped one leg around his ass. He was thicker than most men she'd enjoyed in the past, and she loved the feel as he stretched her to accommodate him. There was nothing quite as pleasurable during sex as the sensation of being truly filled.

"Oh, sweet Lord," he whispered hoarsely, telling her that he, too, was enjoying the feel of them together. She arched her back to take him even deeper and was rewarded by a groan from him that made her smile.

"You feel even better than last night," she said.

"Glad to exceed expectations," he said and kissed her deeply. He probed her mouth with his tongue as his cock did the same to her pussy. When he drove particularly hard, she broke the embrace to gasp her pleasure and he moved his lips down to her breasts, taking a hardened nipple into his mouth and sucking deeply. Pleasure shot through her body, bringing a flood of wetness. "Damn, that's sexy."

"What is?"

"Feeling you drench my cock with your heat."

"What do you think of this?" She flexed the muscles of her pussy to hold him closer.

"Dear God. That feels amazing. You're wrapped so tightly around me."

"You gave me so much pleasure, Drew. Let's see what I can do to make you even harder."

When he pulled back, she lifted her head up to kiss him along his collarbone and tease his nipples with the tip of her tongue. His sighs were soft, but not the gasps she was looking for. When she raked her nails down his back and grabbed his ass, however, he reacted with an involuntary rumble and a surge in his cock as gratifying as it was exciting.

Although he was taller than her, her arms were long. She pushed him up a little and brought her hand between them, caressing the base of his cock where it pressed into her, and teased his balls. Occasionally she played with her clit, knowing her shivers would please him.

"Don't stop," he said.

"I don't intend to," she said and he covered her lips in a bruising kiss. She continued to touch him as he plunged inside of her. She had no trouble finding his rhythm and meeting his thrusts with her hips. She loved moving with a man to increase both their satisfaction.

With her legs wrapped around him, she pulled him closer to her each time he plunged forward, giving them both greater pleasure. She loved being filled by him, watching his passion rise. He was so sexy, so focused on her, his eyes the dark gray of a coming storm.

"Lyria… angel… I'm going to come. I can't hold back."

"I don't want you to. Take your release in me." She increased her attention to his balls and was rewarded with a tightening in his whole body. He rammed into her one final time, and even with the sheath covering him she felt the waves of release rush through him.

He held his body above hers as he came, and she ran her hands gently over his sweat-covered back, enjoying the play of muscles under her fingers. He was strong, yet clearly capable of tenderness. It was a sexy combination.

"I'm in danger of crushing you," he said and rolled gently off her while still holding close.

"Being crushed doesn't sound so bad."

"It is because I will likely want you again later. You are a fire, Lyria. I am so damn drawn to you."

She'd experienced the same pull with him from the first time she saw him but instead of saying anything, she kissed him. He held her closer and she curled against him, listening to the beat of his heart under her ear.

"I am so glad you came back tonight," he said.

"So am I."

* * *

Balban needed to appease his nephew before the younger man blew years of carefully cultivated plans.

Something had happened to the mermaid. Or the Stone. Or both. And the fact that Fiero couldn't find out which or what was making him furious. Two naiads had to be taken to the healing center because of his anger.

"You have got to calm down," his said. "Your fury does not become a leader."

"We have her blood. We have spies in the main compound. We have the contract promising Lyria to me in marriage, but something happened last night either to the Stone of Clarity or to the mermaid and for some reason we cannot get *any* information from any source."

"These things take time."

"And you don't think I've—we've—waited long enough. The mermaids abandoned my mother and me. They deserve to pay for their insolence."

"I don't disagree, but you need to be rational and intelligent no matter the setbacks."

"You're saying I'm not intelligent?"

Damn, his nephew could be so easily rattled. Of course, years of verbal abuse from his nearsighted brother was responsible for that. "You know I don't believe that."

Fiero took a deep breath. And then another. "What should we do?"

"Is the attack on Amina planned and ready to go?"

"Yes, one of the mermaids who is loyal to us, Ulrike, is in place at the main administrative compound. Amina shouldn't recognize her or see anything coming."

"Excellent. The sooner we can initiate this, the better. We'll be closer to having all we need to put all merfolk as well as any Oceanides we desire in their place. Your rule will be undisputed."

A knock at the door interrupted anything Fiero was about to say. A very shaky assistant, this time a female Selkie, entered the room, "Excuse me, sirs. You wanted an update at sundown, which is now."

"Yes, and?"

The Selkie stood there mute. This was not going to be good news. "We have heard nothing new, I'm afraid. New scouts have been sent out within the last hour, but no one has reported back yet."

Fiero walked over to the creature and put his hand on her shoulder. She looked as though she expected him to literally rip her head off. "Thank you for reporting to me when I requested it. I know my anger today has been the cause of concern, and I appreciate your willingness to do as I asked."

The Selkie didn't bother to hide her sigh of relief. "You are most welcome, sir. I promise to check back as soon as we learn something new. Is there anything else you require?"

"Not at this time. You may go."

"Yes, sir. Thank you, sir." She gave a small bow and left the room on legs that were still clearly shaky.

"Well done, son," Balban said. Fiero surprised him. Perhaps the boy was mature enough to see this plan through to the end.

Fiero walked over to his desk, drained the glass of liquid that was there, and threw the glass at the opposite wall where it shattered impressively.

"I know you are frustrated." Fiero shot him a look that was far beyond frustrated. "But Fiero, you have to trust we will get the mermaid, her Stone and the other two stones as well."

"You had better be right, Uncle."

He was. All of Balban's plans relied on it.

Chapter Five

As she turned in his arms, the light from the bedside lamp caught the charms and jewels on her bracelet, especially the large one in the center. He reached out and fingered it. "This is so beautiful and unique. Do you always wear it?"

"Every day since my 18th birthday," she said. "And I've known it would be mine for a long time before that."

Something in her voice suggested sadness, a gravity he didn't understand. "That sounds serious."

"And it's only the beginning."

"Does it signify something?"

"It identifies me as my people's strongest healer."

Her use of the word "people" was odd, as was healer, but some cultures thought that way. "So you're a doctor and didn't have a choice about becoming one?"

"Yes," she said.

"Sounds like quite a challenge for an 18-year-old, not just the position but having to take a job you didn't really want."

"It was. Is. When I started I wasn't very good at it," she said, "but I learned quickly."

"Trial by fire."

"Something like that. My grandmother was the last to wear it. My father's older brother had no daughters so it came to me. I will wear it until I die or until I feel the time is right to pass it to my eldest daughter or closest female relative."

He didn't like her reference to death. She sounded so matter-of-fact about it. As though it were a possibility sooner rather than later. "Did your grandmother help you?"

He saw the sadness in her eyes and regretted asking. "No, she died the year before I was old enough to wear it, but once she knew it would be mine, she taught and showed me what she could."

"I'm sorry. I'm guessing you miss her."

"I do. She was more mother to me than my own."

"I can understand. Angelo Vardini, the owner of The Siren, was more of a father to me than my dad."

"I suppose we are lucky there was someone to love us and take a close interest in us."

He nodded rather than try to talk over the sudden lump in his throat. He understood the loneliness in her voice. He had experienced it on too many occasions when he was younger. Most of the time he thought it made him independent. Sometimes, he just wished for a good friend.

Wanting to shift his thoughts back to her he said, "I assume it's been in your family for a long time?"

"Generations. Each bearer adds either a charm or a jewel to one of the strands. It is believed that it helps in passing down the wisdom from one healer to the next."

"Sounds like a special tradition."

She nodded.

91

"I never wanted to be what my family—well, my father—wanted me to be."

"Which was?"

"A copy of my brother."

"Was that always the case?"

"I don't know. I guess I first noticed it when I was around 13 and my brother got a spot on the varsity team. He was a jock, big on the football team and popular with the girls."

"You didn't want that?"

He laughed. "The girls part, yes. The side of him always placating our father, staying here and do nothing other work in construction and have enough money for beer, steak, and occasional trips to Atlantic City? Not at all. I went on a school trip to New York City in the eighth grade and everything changed. My father never left the area so even though New York isn't far, we never went. He's a small minded man who was happy with a small life. I wanted the big city, the big money, and the big life. Never got along much with him after then."

"Do you miss it? Being close to him?"

Drew didn't answer right away. It wasn't something he thought about. Didn't let himself think about it. "I'm not certain. Back then, no. I was glad to have a different plan from them, no matter how often my father tried to talk me out of it."

"And now?"

"Now I don't have a lot of answers." He kissed her deeply and used the action as a segue to change the subject. "I do have a question for you, however."

"Which is?"

"Will you stay the night with me?"

* * *

It wasn't the first time she received an invitation to spend the night, but she rarely accepted it, and Drew was her first human. Still, this was to be such a limited visit and she wanted as many memories of Drew as she could have to take back with her when it was time to leave.

"I will," she said. *What could it hurt?* she thought and hoped she was right.

* * *

Friday, one day before the full moon.

From the light coming into his bedroom, Lyria figured it was late morning. She smiled and stretched, liking the soreness of a night of passion. Thinking about Drew reminded her that he thought she was a doctor. She didn't like the deception, but it was a little hard to explain to a human that her healing came mostly from magic and not years of school as human healers needed. Still, it was a necessary deception. It went along with not telling him of her Oceanides heritage.

And in four days it wouldn't matter if he thought she was a doctor or a dress maker. She'd be gone.

Rolling over, she saw she was alone. She took a deep breath and smelled something good. She found her way to the kitchen where Drew was cooking and taking frequent drinks out of a large mug. When he saw her, he froze.

"You're naked," he said.

"And you have an unusual way of saying good morning."

"Good morning. You're still naked."

"You seem to have a thing about women's clothes. Or is it just me? First my underwear, now my dress."

"True, you just don't seem to mind at all which I've never experienced with a woman."

She shrugged. "You've already seen me naked. I didn't think it would be a problem. I could put my dress back on if you want."

"Nope, no, no need." She laughed at his repetition. "Don't bother on my account," he said with a smile. "Would you like some coffee?"

She'd heard about humans and coffee, but never tried it herself. "Is it good?"

He looked at her as if her nose were upside down. "You've never tried it?" She shook her head. "It's a gift from the gods." She doubted that. She knew that pleasant gifts were rarely blessed. Ironic, now that she thought about it.

"No, but I'd like to."

"Do you prefer bitter, or sweet and creamy?"

She batted her eyelashes. "Sweet and creamy."

He laughed and handed her a mug, a bowl with sugar and a container of something which said heavy cream. "You may not need coffee like us mere mortals. You already wake up pretty lively."

She poured a little of each into the black liquid, took a sip and added more of both. Two more tries and it was just right. "Strong stuff, but I like it"

"I don't have much for breakfast, although according to the clock, it's almost closer to lunch."

"If you have any fruit that would be perfect for me."

"Not a problem," he said, and presented her with a bowl filled with several different varieties.

"You have dragon fruit," she said, surprised.

"Yeah, it came in unexpectedly the other day and my chef was annoyed because he didn't know what to do with it. I brought it up here until I could figure out what to do with it. I've seen it before, but never tried it."

"It's easy." Most of the food she ate was what Amina said humans called "whole food." Fruits, vegetables and protein in the form of fish. The sea— and the land—had an endless bounty. There was no need to manufacture or modify food. "Do you have a knife?"

He handed her one. She cut off the top, to reveal a thick layer of pink skin with a white speckled core. "Looks like vanilla bean ice cream. It's pretty."

"Isn't it? You cut away a part of the skin, and once it's off you can basically unwrap the skin, almost like a banana."

"Then what?"

"You slice it and feed it to your lover."

"This is my kind of fruit," he said and leaned forward so she could put a piece in his mouth. "It's good. Mild. I wonder if there's a way to put it on the menu. It's not strong enough to go with anything like chocolate, but it could go with sorbet. Or fish. It would certainly look nice on the plates. May I slice you a piece?"

"Absolutely," she said, and opened her mouth.

"Oh, that is way too tempting." He placed a slice on her tongue and then covered her mouth with his. She didn't even consider holding back the sigh. The taste of the fruit mixed with the man was heady.

The rest of the meal continued with him feeding her cereal and her slicing fruit for them both. By the time they were done, they were both sticky and sated. At least for food.

He licked her fingers then continued holding her hand. "Join me in the shower?"

"I'd love to," she said. She didn't tell him this would be another first for her. She'd never spent a night followed by a morning with someone, so no one had ever invited her to shower together, and as much as she loved the occasional warm or hot bath, showers weren't necessary for her.

With a smile she followed him into the bathroom.

* * *

Drew turned on the water and took off his shirt and shorts. It was odd to have her already naked. Odd, but extremely pleasurable. And something he didn't mind getting used to. He pulled an extra towel from the closet; then, looking at her beautiful long red hair, pulled out another.

After checking the water, he offered her his hand and brought her into the stall with him. She let out a sigh. "Is it too hot? I have a tendency to like them hotter than most people. Or so I've been told."

"No, it's heavenly," she said and closed her eyes. Her expression was one of sheer delight and he felt himself hardening.

After they were both wet, he turned her back to him, poured some shampoo in his hands, and began to wash her hair.

"I was wrong," she said.

"About what?"

"That is heavenly."

"Hasn't anyone ever washed your hair for you?"

She shook her head. "It's wonderful."

He kissed her shoulder and continued working the soap through her long strands. She had the longest hair of any woman he'd ever known, and he loved the sensual way it fell over her body and flowed through his fingers. She arched her back in response. Noticing the suds cascading everywhere, he took the opportunity to slide his hands over her body, and when he stroked her breasts with his hands, she let out a sound almost like a purr.

"My turn," she said after he rinsed her hair.

She offered him the same treatment, and he understood her responses. She faced him as she reached up to massage his scalp and her touch sent tingles through his body. He couldn't stop himself from kissing her and licking the water dripping down to her nipples. They hardened under his attention, and when he sucked them deeply, she moaned.

As he rinsed the shampoo out of his hair, he grabbed the soap and covered them both. She wiggled against him, playful and sensual. He couldn't get enough of touching her.

"I need you back in my bed."

She kissed him and pushed him under the spray, following him so they were quickly free of suds. He wrapped her in a towel as she rubbed the other over her hair. After drying himself, he led her back to the bedroom and kissed her until she fell backwards on the bed.

He was already hard from the shower and when

he reached for her pussy he found her slick for him. "I love how quickly you respond."

"You make it easy," she said.

They were close enough to the edge of the bed that he was able to continue kissing her while opening the drawer of his night table to find a condom. He hardly wanted to let go of her to put it on, but when she raked her nails down his back, his need grew and he couldn't wait to be inside her. Turning onto his side, he ripped open the package and protected himself. As he moved to roll on top of her, she pushed herself back on the bed and spread her legs. It was an invitation most men would die for.

He covered her completely, his cock nestled between them. She reached for him, wrapped her hands around his cock, and guided it inside of her. He moaned and took her mouth as he slid into her. Lifting her hips as she had the night before, she met his thrusts and continued to do so until they both groaned with pleasure and his orgasm had him crying out her name.

"I've never known a woman as sensual as you," he said, holding her as their heartbeats returned to normal.

"I'm glad it pleases you."

"An understatement if I ever heard one," he said, kissing her.

They stepped out of the shower and he wrapped her in a towel as she finger combed her hair. Damn, she looked so sweet. He couldn't help himself, he kissed her nose and she giggled. Before he could do more his phone, which he'd left on the side of the sink, beeped with the notice of a text message. He ignored it and continued drying her, rubbing her skin and kissing where he exposed.

It buzzed again twice more. He hated moving away from her, but he reached for the annoying piece of technology that would continue to pester him until he answered it. He read the message from downstairs and groaned. "Playtime's over. Time to get downstairs. Afternoon shift will be gearing up and I have to be certain we have what we need for the evening. Friday nights are crazy. Both of my lead chefs are working: one for the club food and desserts, one for the main dining room. Having them both working is going to lead to additional problems. I need to go in and do whatever is necessary to keep the carnage to a minimum, my beauty."

"I don't know what it takes to make a restaurant kitchen run, but I've witnessed the dynamic of two strong leaders battling over the same territory. There's usually a lot of arguing and everyone needs to be willing to compromise to some extent."

"Compromise. Yeah, there's a vocabulary word I need to teach them. Maybe I should post the definition over the stove area."

"How is it you have two lead chefs? It can't possibly work well."

"It doesn't, which is another reason I need to be there—for the first round of fighting. And the second." He sighed and rubbed his hands over his face. "And possibly the third."

"Shouldn't you just fire one? Or have them work different shifts?"

"If only it were that simple."

"Isn't it?"

"Unfortunately not. There aren't a lot of jobs out there, especially year-round ones, and Mr. V. was loyal to them both. Part of the condition of my taking the job was not firing either of them. He was able to make it work and keep the peace. Unfortunately, I don't have his magic touch when it comes to diplomacy."

"My cousin Amina is the peacekeeper in our family. She'd like your Mr. V. People seem to want to listen to her and accept her suggestions. Even me. I don't know how she does it, but one moment I can be arguing and then with a few well-placed comments and sentences, everything is well again. May I join you there? Maybe I can find way of helping, or at least keep the waters calm."

He smiled at her. "I'd like that. No matter what, it will be a nicer evening if you're close."

* * *

"There are some things I need to take care of this afternoon, and I should change my dress, but I'll join you shortly after sundown." She'd been thinking about how to make use of her time on land and had a plan

"You'll be okay on your own?"

Didn't he trust her? Or was this a natural male concern? It frustrated her when she couldn't tell. Humans were supposed to be so easy for her to read. This one was not. She wondered why. Of course, given her attack the other night, maybe his worry was well founded. "I'll be fine."

"Okay." He put his arms around her and kissed her deeply. "I know this is very forward of me, but considering all we've already shared in the last day, would you consider staying with me for the rest of your visit?"

"Here? Stay here? Live here?"

"Why not?"

The reasons 'why not' were numerous, or at least she thought they must be, but she couldn't think of any. It would only be for a few days. No harm could come of it, she decided, and she would like the memories to have in the future. "Sounds lovely. Can I bring my things over from the motel?"

"Absolutely. We'll keep them in my office until we come home."

Come home. He made it sound like a long term arrangement. She didn't know how she felt about that. "I can do that." She thought she kept the concern out of her voice.

"Good, it's settled and I'll see you at The Siren later."

It wasn't until after she was back in her motel room that the voice of sanity—sounding suspiciously like Amina—said, "Are you losing you mind?"

Although it had only been a day, Lyria hoped it was all she was losing.

After getting a map from a tourist kiosk and asking for some help, Lyria took a bus to the stop closest to the library. She might be trapped here for a while, but it didn't mean she couldn't try to find a solution or at least some information while she was here. Humans had different information sources and references from Oceanides, and she though perhaps there could be an unexpected solution among their sources.

She marveled at her own ability to get around the town of Point Pleasant. It was unexpectedly fun. She had never stayed on land long enough to see anything other than the coastline and even that she didn't explore much. People here were friendly and there was a wide mix of ages from children to young mothers with babies in strollers to older couples walking hand in hand after decades of companionship. Having this kind of contact with and exposure to humans was not as disconcerting as she'd feared it would be, and she was enjoying her interactions with them. She might even miss it after she left.

After getting a lesson from the librarian on using the internet and online catalog, she searched for books on sea magic and crystals. Amina had told her about the internet, but she didn't understand her cousin's interest. Now that she was able to access an outrageous amount of information quickly and easily, she could see the appeal. She could find information from all corners of the world, new and old.

She looked up information on colored sapphires and didn't find much beyond what she already knew. It was mined all over the world and was very popular in jewelry. Humans associated it with joy, peace and beauty as well as considered it a strong gem for healing. It was also believed to have strong energy for general protection as well as protection from evil. The other night certainly showed that to be the case. Lyria marveled at how close they actually were to the truth of the powers within the gem, especially the Stone of Clarity.

It was unfortunate, she thought, that humans weren't generally attuned to the magic around them, the support available for them to tap into. Still, she supposed this blindness kept her people relegated to fairy tales and safe from probing dangers of the humans they shared the world with.

Although she didn't expect much, she was sorry to discover that with all the legends and stories of her world, there was no hidden truth to help her learn how to shield the Stone of Clarity from someone who sought it or how to locate the central realm of the Sea Dragon. In fact, most of her searches using the phrase 'sea dragon' resulted in images of a tiny water creature that bore no resemblance to Fiero—or a listing of Asian and fish restaurants.

Still, reading through the different legends and tales as well as stories of how humans treated the unknown, different and unfamiliar vividly reminded her that it was one thing to have fun with someone of another race, but it was another thing entirely to try to create anything permanent and long term. It led to problems, heartache and more loss than she wanted to contemplate.

Although almost immediately after she remembered the fun and pleasure she shared with Drew, as well as the pleasure she anticipated for the evening. He really was a wonderful male and she enjoyed their time together. She liked listening to him, talking with him.

But it was only for fun, she reminded herself. She couldn't share her whole truth with him. He'd never believe. Never accept.

She slammed the lore and legends book shut. She could not allow her thoughts to go in this direction, and certainly not her feelings. Looking out at the sun, she decided it was time to head back to the boardwalk, get her things from the hotel then grab a late lunch before heading to see Drew.

* * *

Lyria arrived at The Siren a little after five. When he saw her, Drew thought it was his first smile in hours. The restaurant was just starting to get busy with families with little children and older couples. The club would be quiet until at least eight and Drew said this was the best time for them to grab a quick bite to eat. He fixed them two salads and fish and chips. It was Lyria's first experience with fried foods and Drew was delighted by her reaction. So much to her was new and although he couldn't understand how she hadn't experienced so much. He wondered where she came from and how she lived, but mostly he enjoyed watching her react. It made him aware of how jaded he had allowed himself to become. He found himself looking at things from her perspective. When he did, he appreciated how good the meal tasted and made a mental note to add malt vinegar to the table settings.

As they were finishing up, they were, of course, interrupted.

"Boss, I don't mean to alarm you," Jody, one of his servers, said in a tone which immediately told him he should probably be alarmed. "But Todd didn't come in today and after one customer too many complained, Stanley walked out."

It was on the tip of his tongue to say, "You've got to be kidding," but it would have been a waste of time and energy, and he was clearly going to need both. As if Friday nights weren't busy enough. "Come with me," he said to Lyria and grabbed her hand as he made a beeline for the kitchen.

Chaos reigned. Servers fought over orders to be

brought out, food burned on the stove, and Neil, the kid hired to assist Stanley and Todd, looked ready to cry or quit. Maybe both.

Drew cleared his throat and in his loudest voice he said, "Everyone, freeze." It was gratifying to watch all movement stop. He took a deep breath and a quick inventory of the situation before continuing. "Okay, this is a shitty position to be in, no question, but we will deal with it because we have no choice, and we will be successful because that's the best possible outcome. The first thing to do is get our customers served so they come back again. And tip well tonight. Right?" There were nods of agreement. "So, the wait staff is going to let our guests know there's been a delay in the kitchen and offer everyone dessert and coffee on the house. If they don't want it tonight, we'll give them gift certificates for their next visit."

"What a great idea," said Jody. "It will encourage them to come back even if they didn't have the best experience tonight."

"Exactly. While you are doing that, I am going to review the orders we have so far and start cooking so we can complete them as efficiently as possible." When he finished speaking, everyone was still standing there. He smiled when he realized why. They were waiting for him to tell them what to do next. He couldn't remember the last time anyone waited on his word. "Let's move and make it a good night, no matter what."

And they did.

He walked to the stoves, gave Neil a squeeze on the shoulder. "You and I are going to work together, kid, and it's going to be fine. Trust me?"

"Yes, sir, Mr. Crawford."

"Good. And it's Drew, definitely not sir." When Neil managed a smile, Drew had his first moment of hope for the night. It wasn't going to be easy, but it was possible. "Lyria, can you cook or do food prep?"

She shook her head. "Not in the least, but if any of your servers know how to, I can take their place with the customers and let them work back here with you."

After a quick poll of the staff he learned Jody recently finished her second year of hotel management school and she was thrilled to join Drew and Neil at the stoves. It took more than an hour before they weren't ridiculously behind, but soon after the worst had passed and they were caught up, accepting new orders without concerns or delays. He breathed a sigh of relief when his hostess came in to tell him they were down to only a 25-minute wait out front, normal for this time on a Friday. Looking around at the now efficiently running kitchen, he grabbed a towel, wiped the sweat from his face and smiled. He had done it. They had done it. It felt good to work as a part of a team.

As Jody offered him a plate that needed its main course, he said, "You must be acing your classes." She was dynamite. Professional and orderly, she learned quickly, took direction well, and was able to keep up the pace as the evening wore on.

"I'm doing well, but I have to say I've never had quite this level of hands-on experience."

"No substitute for the real thing, is there?"

"Definitely not, and I really like it."

Without thinking he said, "Me too." Then it was

his turn to freeze. The realization hit him hard. Not including the night Lyria arrived, this was the first time he enjoyed being at The Siren since returning. When he looked at the clock, he couldn't believe how much time had passed, instead of dragging as it frequently did. He completely forgot about the routines that filled each day, making him bored and restless and convinced that as soon as Mr. V. was back on his feet, Drew was hitting the road again.

"We're getting compliments on your bacon meatloaf, Drew," said Lyria, bringing him out of his troubling thoughts. "I have a feeling it's going to need to be a permanent item on the menu, or at least a regular special, the way people keep ordering and enjoying it."

"Glad to hear it."

When Drew started to make sense of the orders they'd received, it became clear they were not going to have enough for several of the regular menu items. He had a feeling Todd didn't come in because he didn't place the requisitions to stock the kitchen, which may also have contributed to Stanley's frustrations.

A quick inventory of what was available in the freezer and pantry didn't give Drew a lot of options, but he was able to add the bacon meatloaf along with a light pasta dish with crabmeat and vegetables as alternatives. He completely lucked out on having a good stock of desserts, but when things calmed down he'd sent Neil up the road to the local diner known for its baked goods just in case they started to run low.

It had been years since he'd worked in the kitchen and never during the dinner rush on a Friday night. Mr. V. used to let him do prep work alongside Nico on

Mondays when things were slowest as he taught them some of the secrets of his recipes. Drew wished Nico was with him now, working side by side. It would have been fun. Of course, if Nico hadn't been killed, there would have been no need for Drew to come.

Life was a series of unexpected changes, Drew thought, and there wasn't a damn thing you could do about them except—like a wave—ride them out or get completely tumbled. He wasn't sure which choice he'd made, but for the first time in a while, he felt as though he were riding.

"How are you managing on the floor?" he asked Lyria

She looked confused. "I'm not doing anything to the floor."

"Ah, you have to get used to restaurant slang. The floor is a reference to the dining area."

"I thought there was a language I wasn't getting. Can you tell me what a four top is?"

"A table with four place settings."

"Got it," she said. "I'm picking up things on the floor pretty quickly, although two tops are easier than four."

"Well said. And good job. Sorry to make you work on your vacation."

"It's not a problem. I'm actually having fun. I like helping out."

"Good, because we definitely needed the help." He held out a hand, and when she took it, he pulled her close for a kiss.

"That's my kind of tip," she said, when he let her go. "I'm going to want more later."

"I'll be happy to give them to you."

"I will be happy to receive them." She blew him one last kiss as she headed back out to the tables.

At 10:00 the main kitchen was officially closed and they offered only bar food until 1:00 a.m. The serving staff reset the tables for lunch the next day, gave Drew feedback on what worked, what didn't, and what they thought might help. He noticed they looked surprised when he asked their opinions and pleased when he took them seriously. No one knew the front of the house better than the wait staff, a truth he'd learned from experience, and he was glad to get their input.

When the last of the staff left, only he and Lyria remained in the kitchen. The menu for the rest of the night was appetizers, something he could manage on his own.

"You made them feel really good," Lyria said, coming up behind him and putting her arms around him.

"Who?"

"Your employees, when you asked for their thoughts. It was a great thing to do."

He was about to brush off the compliment, but instead he let it sink in. "You know this is the first time I feel like I've done anything good for anyone in ages. I didn't even think about it. It came naturally, but now I can see where I gave them a chance to be taken seriously and I got feedback which will help make things work better around here."

"A winning combination," she said.

"Sorry it wasn't quite the night you had planned."

"Don't be. I had fun. I met lots of people, which I love doing. Your servers are a fun group, and I got to see you having a great time."

So she saw it, too. He didn't quite know how to take it. Part of him was pleased, but part also feared it would be a one-shot deal, a novelty evening and nothing further.

By 2:00, the last of the bar and dance patrons were gone and the place was closed. Drew was still on such a high from the night. He couldn't believe how much fun he'd had or how smoothly everything had gone. He had too much energy to even think about going to sleep, not to mention being too sweaty to want to go near his sheets.

As they walked out, he asked, "Up for a quick swim?"

"Absolutely," Lyria said, and took his hand. At the door, they pulled in different directions.

"Where are you going?" he said.

"To the beach. Where are you going?"

"To the apartment to get a suit."

"Why bother? Let's just plunge in naked."

"Why bother is right," he said.

They shed their clothes and left them by a pylon under the restaurant's pier, looked around to make certain they were alone, and ran into the waves. The cooling water was heaven against his skin, and he lost himself as he took long strokes out to deeper water, enjoying cutting through the ocean. He stopped when Lyria passed unexpectedly beneath him.

"You little sneak," he said as she surfaced. She looked so beautiful with her wet hair pulled away from her face, wearing nothing but drops of water. He moved to kiss her, but she ducked beneath a wave and disappeared.

Although the moon was nearly full, there were no

lights from the shore and it was difficult to see in the dark. He didn't want to call too loudly for her in case there were people on the beach. Attracting attention while skinny dipping was not a good idea.

Lyria was like a frisky fish in the water. She would pop up to kiss him or touch him, then dart away before he could grab her. She swam around him, under him, even once between his legs—which was stimulating in ways he never would have expected. The feel of her slick skin beneath the water was tantalizing. He was grateful he could touch bottom or she might have pulled him under with all her movement.

On the other hand, he couldn't catch her no matter how hard he tried. He was ready to call a truce when he sensed her at his feet. Making tight circles, she swirled the water around him and swam slowly up his body. By the time her lips were on his, he was fully aroused and aching for her. Her body was cool and slick from the ocean and tasted of salt and something uniquely her. She was more intoxicating than any drink his bartender could create.

He ran his hands over her wet hair and pulled her mouth closer, teasing her tongue with his and relishing her small gasps and moans.

It wasn't enough. Drew put a hand on Lyria's back and arched her away from him, exposing her breasts above the water's surface. He leaned over her and licked at the drops of water, loving how hard her nipples were from excitement and the cool night air. Sucking and pinching them in turn, he increased the sensitivity of the small buds as she wrapped her legs around him to stay close. Her hair floated in the water behind her, and the

111

charms on her bracelet caught the moonlight every so often as she was lifted by the waves.

She looked like a goddess, laid out bare before him, and he couldn't have wanted her more.

* * *

As Drew's excitement rose, his emotions reached out to Lyria and she let down the natural protection she had against the feelings of others. She was aroused enough on her own, but when she added his to the mix, she thought she might orgasm without any additional touching. She'd never experienced how two people's feelings, how the connection, could grow. It intensified everything.

It wasn't smart of her to allow his emotions to touch her. His feelings whirled around her like the ocean. As thrilling as it was unnerving, she feared it might make it difficult for her to keep things between them about physical pleasure and nothing beyond. She considered for a moment, then decided not to worry. She would be gone before anything meaningful developed. If his pleasure added to hers, why not enjoy it while she could?

She bent forward, tightened her legs around him, and kissed him, taking in his hunger and desire. Tonight she witnessed a new side of him. She wasn't certain he was aware of it, but he was happier and more relaxed under the demands in the kitchen than he was at any other time she'd seen him. True, they'd known each other for less than three days, which wasn't a lot to base her conclusion on, but she sensed a change in him which he needed and was long overdue.

Running her hands down his back, she enjoyed the strength of his muscles and she kneaded them, knowing they would be sore from the night's work. His moan was a welcome reward.

His erection brushed her entrance and the tease sent tingles through her body. The combination of cool water and warm skin was heady. She allowed her hands to wrap around his waist, then down to his ass, loving the way the different muscle groups changed and moved. Men's bodies were so lusciously different from hers and she loved the variation.

"I could take you here," he said.

"I won't stop you."

"Unfortunately my current outfit doesn't have pockets, so my condoms are back in my wallet, which is lying on the beach."

As much as she didn't want to wait, she appreciated that he wouldn't do anything to cause her injury or an unwanted situation. She could tell him she was certain it wasn't her fertile time—mermaids were well aware of their cycles—but that might require an explanation she didn't want to offer and, one way or another, would spoil the mood.

"Shall we swim back?" she asked.

"Not until after I kiss and touch you for a while longer. I want to drive you completely wild before I even think of taking it further."

He was as good as his word. As they kissed, he caressed her breasts, her ass, and her pussy, teasing her into a frenzy of desire. It had been a long time since someone took her pleasure into account, especially before their own.

Her past really wasn't filled with former lovers

and in fact there were only two she stayed involved with for any length of time, and none since Wilmar.

Memories of him still stung. She'd been with him for nearly a year and had been wondering if it might lead to something permanent when Amina told her he didn't care about her. He was only using her to gain influence and power, hoping to marry her so his children could have a position of importance in their community. He'd assaulted Amina and was punished. Their nasty break-up was gossip for weeks in various social circles, and he continued to spread rumors about her being cold while also trying to find ways to convince her to come back to him, going so far as to say no other male would be willing to always be second to her work.

Since then Lyria was instantly suspicious of any merman who showed an interest in her, and for years no one had been worth more than a brief encounter to release the urge for sex.

Until Drew.

Who was a human.

And currently driving her insane with the way his fingers were pushing into her. The combination of the cool water and her own warm wetness was tantalizing, adding to the sensations he was already building within her. She touched him everywhere she could, but he made it challenging by keeping her at a fever pitch, distracting her from anything but what he was doing. Finally, he concentrated on the spot deep within her that sent an orgasm crashing through her with almost no warning. She reached for his head and pulled his mouth to hers for a searing kiss to keep her from screaming out her pleasure.

"I love watching you react. God, you look so beautiful."

She was breathing too hard to answer and doubted, for the first time in her life, her ability to swim to shore.

"I've made a woman speechless," he said. "That's good for my ego."

She floated next to him, both literally and figuratively, and they continued to kiss. For this moment, there was no one in the world but the two of them and she was lighter and happier than she could remember being in years. She wanted to focus on nothing but Drew and not think past the next few minutes.

The sand under her feet surprised her. She didn't notice Drew walking them in as they kissed, but she was grateful for the assistance since her legs were still wobbly from her orgasm.

"I've always wanted to do this," he said, kissing her neck and collarbone.

"Kiss naked on the beach?"

"And have sex in the open like this."

"You've never made love on the sand? You grew up here."

"At 18 my skills with women were not smooth, and by the time they had improved, I wasn't here anymore."

"Then I'm glad to help you make a fantasy come true." She dropped to her knees and he joined her. When she saw the condom package in his hand, she took it from him and opened it. "I, on the other hand, have enjoyed it before, and I can tell you without a blanket there really is only one position that works well and keeps sand out of uncomfortable areas."

"Which is?"

"Would it excite you if I were bent forward and on my knees?"

It was a good thing his knees were already bent or her words could have led to an embarrassing situation. Having her offer herself to him was tantalizing beyond any fantasy he'd imagined. Nothing beat the reality of a beautiful woman in front of you.

The way she'd climaxed for him while they were in the water was exquisite and like nothing he'd ever experienced with someone. He would never get over how uninhibited and free she was, expressing and giving. He would have slid into her right then if he didn't worry about keeping her protected.

As soon as he could, he put on a condom. Lyria turned onto all fours, looked over her shoulder, and invited him to take her. He couldn't decide if he wanted to melt or explode at the sight. He could see enough of her face to see the desire there, for him, and the rush that ran through his body made him harder than he already was.

Which he didn't think was possible.

"Don't wait, Drew. I want you now."

He didn't need the encouragement but it was exciting to hear. He positioned himself behind her, grabbed her hips and found her wet opening with the tip of his cock. With a quick forward movement, he was sheathed inside her heat and she clenched the muscles around him, bringing him in deeper.

The feeling was exquisite, made more so by the sound of the waves and the feel of the breeze reminding him they were out in the open, completely exposed. She moved against him, rotating her hips, showing him she didn't care about their environment—only him.

He pulled back, then thrust into her, burying himself in her body. She shivered and her wetness bathed his shaft, encouraging him further while making it easy for him to get as deep as he could.

While part of him wanted to make this last, it wasn't going to be an option. He was already too excited. He increased his pace and she easily picked up his rhythm, moving back against him each time he pushed. When he pulled out, the cool night air teased his cock only to have her warm him a moment later. Leaning forward, he grabbed for her breasts, their fullness even heavier as they swayed with her movements. Her moans of pleasure and cries of "oh, yes!" were all he needed to go completely over the edge.

"Lyria, I'm going to come," he said, trying to be quiet but hoping to be heard.

"Yes, lover, yes. Take your pleasure in me, as I did in you."

He gave a final push as his climax raced through him with a power he'd rarely, if ever, experienced. Grabbing her shoulders, he pushed her toward him, driving him as deeply into her as he could. Lyria arched her back and moaned, then circled her hips, adding to the already amazing sensation.

"Dear God," he said. He dropped his head on her shoulder, and tried not to topple them both onto the sand. After a few deep breaths, he sat back on his heels, bringing her with him. Still semi-erect, he remained in her body, enjoying the rippling aftershocks running through his body. She let her head fall back on his shoulder and he kissed her.

"Did that fulfill your fantasy?"

"That was beyond any fantasy I could have ever imagined."

She smiled. "Oh, good."

"I'm going to have to come up with some other fantasies we can shoot the hell out of."

"Sounds like fun to me."

He kissed her again. "For now, however, we are going to have to find a way to walk back to my apartment."

"Which could be the biggest challenge of the night. Given all that happened this evening, that's saying something."

He decided it could be fun to have more challenges to share and meet with her. After tonight, he wasn't any clearer, but he was definitely hopeful in a way he hadn't been for a long time.

"I don't think I can fall asleep after the night we've had, in and out of The Siren."

"Any ideas?" she asked.

His stomach rumbled in answer, and they laughed "Clearly I have one more appetite that wants to be fed.

"Do you really want to cook so late?"

"No, and there is no need to. You are in the heart of the culinary experience known as the 24-hour diner. Let's go get some breakfast."

"Breakfast? In the middle of the night?"

"Trust me, my lady. You don't know what you're missing."

* * *

They drove to the OB Diner, and Lyria was glad it was close. It was one thing to see automobiles driving by, it was quite another to be in one. She could swim fast, probably faster than Drew was driving, but she was petrified for the entire trip although she tried not to let it show.

"Hey, Drew! Didn't expect to see you in here tonight," a woman called as they walked in. "How'd you end up managing."

"Hi, Tina. Thanks for being there with the desserts tonight. That was crazy beyond words."

"I hear you. We know what it's like to get in the weeds around here. Grab a booth or a table and I'll bring you some menus. Want decaf?"

"Sounds good, thanks."

He walked Lyria over to a booth with ketchup, mustard, salt, pepper, sugar and packages of jelly already on the table along with paper mats at each seat. "In the weeds?" she asked.

"It's an expression meaning completely overwhelmed and behind in filling orders and helping customers. It's the situation we found ourselves in tonight."

Tina came over with two mugs of coffee and little cups of creamer. She placed the menus in front of them and said, "And we were there to bail you out with a few extra desserts."

"That you were. What would we have done without your rice pudding and chocolate cream pie?"

"I shudder to think, darling."

"Anything we can do to help in the future, just ask."

She gave him a wink and walked off to help a group of young adult males who looked to have enough food on the table to feed twice as many people.

"There's nothing fancy about this place," Drew said, "but the food is great and served in abundance."

They opened up their menus and looked through. Lyria couldn't believe the number of pages of items they had. The menu at The Siren wasn't in half this big. "I don't know where to start."

"Do you trust me?"

That was a loaded question, but since she knew what he meant, she said yes. When Tina came back he said, "Two orders of hash and eggs over easy and a double stack of banana pancakes." Tina didn't even bother to write down what he said. Lyria was impressed. Having spent the night waiting tables, she didn't think she could do that. "I hope you're hungry," Drew said.

"Not surprisingly, I am," she said.

As they waited for their order Lyria took in the décor. The place was a good size but it wasn't busy at the moment. Given the size of the menu, however, she could imagine that during regular meal times it was a madhouse. In addition to the tables in the center and the booths on the side, there was a long counter, not unlike the bar back at the club. Two men were sitting there arguing over something called the Mets. She didn't know what or who they were but it was clearly very important. At the end of the counter she could see a refrigerated case filled with desserts.

Drew must have seen her looking because he said, "Maybe we should have started with something sweet."

She laughed. "No, what you ordered sounded good." Actually she had no idea if it was good at all and quite frankly she was a little nervous about something called 'hash' but she was willing to go along with his choices.

It wasn't long before Tina came back balancing four plates. She put the hash and eggs in front of them and the two plates of pancakes with bananas on them in the center of the table. "Need anything else?"

"A bigger appetite?" Lyria suggested.

Tina laughed. "I'll package up anything you don't finish."

Lyria took a deep breath. It all smelled wonderful. "Now what??

"Follow my lead." Drew broke up the eggs which were laid on top of the hash letting the yokes run everywhere. When he'd thoroughly tossed them together he squirted ketchup all over in a zig-zag design.

Lyria had tried ketchup when one of the other servers offered her some French fries during their shift, but she couldn't see herself drowning the poor dish with them, so she copied Drew but used less ketchup.

Meanwhile he spread butter on the pancakes and between the layers and then gave them a light dowsing with a brown liquid. "I'm not going to put too much syrup on them in case you don't like a lot, but I'm telling you now—I'm going to be adding lots more to each one of my bites. Fair warning."

He dove into the hash first and so she followed. She started chewing and stopped. The textures, the taste were all so different, so new. It was salty and savory. The eggs and the ketchup added a smoothness. It was like nothing she'd ever had, and it was so very good. She didn't realize she was eating fairly quickly until Drew said, "I guess you were hungry."

Lyria looked at her plate to see that more than half of the food was gone. "It's wonderful."

"Try the pancakes." He cut a piece for her, slicing

the knife through all three and serving her a three level wedge. She opened her mouth and let him feed her. Now she was assaulted with a completely different set of tastes—smooth, sweet, warm, even a little slippery with the banana cooked inside.

She sighed. "It's amazing."

"Yup, nothing like breakfast in the middle of the night."

"I have to admit, you're right. I never would have imagined it, but it's perfect."

They made quick work of their meal, talking about the night and a little bit about what would be necessary the next day. He warned her that Saturdays were tough.

"I think we can handle anything after tonight."

He took her hand and kissed it. "With you by my side, I believe that."

The pancake she'd been swallowing got stuck in her throat. She couldn't stay by his side, couldn't let him hope. Before she could say something, Tina was back.

"Guess you don't need those to-go containers after all," she said.

"Nope. Once I start, you know I can't stop."

"That's our goal. Glad you enjoyed it."

She had, but now her thoughts were about trying to stop Drew from thinking of them too much as a couple. Unfortunately, she couldn't think of anything to say that wouldn't completely ruin their night.

There would be enough time to say something tomorrow. She was smart enough not let things get out of control.

And smart enough not to leave any of her pancakes uneaten.

Chapter Six

Saturday, Full Moon

After their late night, it was close to noon before they woke up. Drew realized he was hungry again. First for the woman in his bed, which was an ideal way to wake up, and then for food. While Lyria finished getting dressed, he looked in his refrigerator and through cupboards and decided grilled cheese with tomato would be good.

As he buttered toast and listened to her in the other room he could hardly believe they'd only met on Wednesday night. He'd dated women for months and never felt this comfortable with them. Or happy. With her there was a connection, an awareness of everything around him and himself. For months he'd been guarded and reserved. Shut down. Maybe it had been longer than that. Since he arrived back in New Jersey, he'd ended every day thinking about being one day closer to leaving town.

Last night, his final thoughts were of her.

This morning he woke up happy to be where he was, due in part to the great night they had at The Siren, but also due in large part to Lyria. Her visit was only supposed to last until Tuesday, but he wanted — needed—to find a way to have her stay longer. It might not be fair to ask, since he wasn't certain how much longer he would be here, but every day with her was worth it. If she was willing to extend her time, then perhaps she'd also be willing to go with him when he left.

The sizzle of butter brought him out of his thoughts. How strange was it for him to be looking for ways to keep her in his life? A few days ago his run-in with his brother reminded him about the dangers of trust and close ties, but today it didn't seem nearly as dangerous as not having time to be with Lyria.

* * *

After making love, Lyria took a little time to get ready, brushing out her hair—not a quick task—and pulling it back with combs. She met him in the kitchen where whatever he was making smelled good, but looked odd. She was getting used to that.

"Good morning again," he said and kissed her when she got close. "Are you hungry?"

"I am," she said, "which is surprising considering how much I ate last night."

"Well, we did start the day burning more calories."

"Yes, that's one way to put it. What are you making?"

"Grilled cheese with tomato. It's good with bacon too but I'm all out of bacon. This will have to do."

"I'm sure it will be great. I've loved everything you've served me so far." He wiggled his eyebrows at her and she laughed. "Yes, even that."

"This falls under the category of comfort food. In the winter it's particularly good with soup. I think you'll like it. Trust me."

Trust. There was that word. Her mind said not to open even the smallest door that might create a lasting connection, but when her stomach growled and the smell of the food reached her, she decided this was barely a window, let alone a door. She opened her mouth and he fed her the sandwich.

She was first struck by the crunchy toast—bread was one of those foods humans had that was enviable. She did purchase it on occasion—then by the warm melted cheese and the subtle sweetness of the tomatoes. For something so simple it was quite delicious.

"Do you like it?"

"Mhm," she said, still enjoying the flavor.

"Glad you tried it?"

"Definitely," she said. As they continued to eat, she noticed he was staring at her. "Is something wrong?"

"What's in your hair?"

"Combs. I know they're old-fashioned but it's one of the only things that works to hold my hair back. Is there something wrong with them?

"Not at all. They're beautiful, but even though they're unusual, I'm pretty certain I've seen one like it before."

"You have?" she said, concerned

"Yes, a little girl once found one in the ocean. She almost drowned and she claimed a lady in the water had saved her and given her the comb. I assumed it had something to do with her being scared and almost dying, but it's odd to see another one so similar to hers."

Lyria remembered. She'd given one up a long time ago to the girl who nearly lost her life to the sea. Since he'd been the one to save her, she should have considered he might have seen the comb she pressed into the little one's hand as a means of comfort and reassurance. Thankfully, his version of the story wasn't quite accurate. "I hope she was okay," Lyria said.

He nodded. "It was my last day here before heading out to college, my last save of the summer. Actually, my last save ever."

"What do you mean?"

"I left for college the next day. As soon as I picked up my final paycheck I packed up and left as fast as my old Civic could take me. I haven't been back for more than a weekend since then. Well, until March, when Mr. Vardini called and asked me to run The Siren while he was out of commission."

"You said you really didn't like it here. Wasn't there anything good?"

He shrugged. "I liked aspects of it. Had a friend or two I missed. Nico, Mr. Vardini's son, was one of them, but he died in Kabul."

"I'm so sorry," Lyria said. She was familiar with war and the losses it led to. It was one of the reasons she had to keep the Stone from Fiero. Too many creatures would rise to fight him and lose if he gained the power he wanted. Too many innocent people would die. That almost happened because of her once before and she vowed never again. "Where did you move to?"

"Chicago. It's where I went to college and grad school. Then after working at a few different companies, I started a management consulting and sales business out there with a so-called friend from business school. That didn't work out like I thought either. Seems I'm not very good at making plans."

Lyria took his hand in hers. "Then there must be a different plan in store for you."

"I suppose. Still, I never expected to be back here. Never wanted to, but Mr. V.'s closer to me than my own family, so when he needed me, I came."

"Your business didn't need you?"

"There was nothing left. My partner sold plans and strategies of ours to a competitor, then went to work for them, leaving me holding a worthless business with a lot of debt. Mr. V. called only a few weeks after it all went to hell, when I was still trying to figure out what to do with my life. This gave me something to do. A way to at least be valuable to someone."

Lyria wondered if it was really a coincidence or if this man had found a way to take care of someone who was special to him. Something told her it might be the latter.

* * *

"That was wonderful," she said closing her eyes with a smile as she finished her sandwich. He might have been jealous if it weren't for the fact his kisses could make her look as pleased and satisfied. "I'm full."

"I'm glad you liked it. It did turn out pretty well," he said as he finished his own meal. "Hopefully we can keep all our customers happy for the rest of the

127

weekend until I can start a search for some new cooks. This time, cooks with smaller egos."

"I don't understand you," she said.

He put his plate in the sink then turned and stared at her. That came out of nowhere. "What don't you understand?"

"You love to cook and you do it very well."

"I do, and thank you."

"And you run a club with a restaurant, where the chefs have abandoned you and left the kitchen in your hands."

"Yes."

"And you have no other specific plans for the future?"

"Where are you going with this?" He had an idea, but didn't really like it.

"Why don't you get in the kitchen and run it yourself? It seems as though it's a perfect fit."

Drew grabbed an apple from a bowl and took a large bite, filling his mouth and stalling for time. It wasn't as if he hadn't thought about taking over in there, especially on some of the nights when he was about ready to kill Todd and Stanley. Now, with them gone, he had free reign ere. Lyria was right. He enjoyed cooking. It was creative and fun. But to make it his job? And stay here permanently? It was out of the question. He had a college and a business degree. That meant not sweating all day behind a stove. Not being at the whims of the economy, the tourist season or the latest boardwalk fads.

Didn't it?

"It's really not what I want to be doing."

"Oh, I'm surprised."

"Why?"

"Because the other night when Stanley walked out and you took over, that was the happiest I've seen you look, not including when we have sex." Drew almost spit out the juice he was trying to swallow. "Which, by the way, was incredible last night, even though you should have been completely exhausted and drained and would have been if you hadn't enjoyed yourself so much and felt so successful."

Her candor was usually wonderful, but in the moment it was not what he was ready for or what he wanted to hear. But unfortunately, she was right. Last night was the first night at The Siren where the time flew by and at the end of the night he felt as though he had put in a good day's work.

A good day's work. He remembered his father's expression, usually used in reference to a day when business was busy. Drew never wanted that kind of day. He wanted something bigger and grander, and it had landed him right back where he started, no happier than when he began. In fact, he was more jaded and less sure of himself than he had been in years.

Except when he was cooking.

It completely focused him while simultaneously taking him out of himself. It was easy for him to see what dishes were popular, what was never being ordered, and since March, he'd had an idea or two for new recipes he would offer if he ran the kitchen.

Which he didn't.

But he could.

"Am I wrong in what I saw?"

"No, although I wish I could say you were."

"Why would you wish that?" He thought she

sounded angry. "There is something you love to do, something you want to do, and you have the opportunity to do it. Why, in the name of the seas and skies, would you wish it were not true? Do you know how many people would give anything to be able to do what they wanted or loved?"

Yes, definitely angry. He would have to ask her about that later. "You're right. I didn't think of it that way and I see your point, but it's a lot for me to wrap my head around. I've been picturing this this as temporary, not a career decision."

"Is there something else you want for your career?"

"Absolutely. I had a very clear picture of what I wanted. My own business which would also include power, respect, and more income than I knew I probably deserved. I got them, too"

"And you expected that career and the things that came with it would make you happy."

He nodded.

"Did they?"

"They did for quite a while. It was fun. Sort of. Then, like I said, someone I thought I could trust lied to me and single-handedly destroyed everything we'd built together. After, I didn't know how to start again. I didn't trust myself." Ouch, that hurt to say out loud.

"Which is why you returned?"

"Yes. Mr. V. was always someone I trusted and who trusted me, even though we met because I told a lie about his son." Drew explained the story of teasing Nico and coming to the Vardini household to make amends. "This time I was on the receiving end of the lie, but no one was coming to apologize or help. After being stabbed in the back …"

His voice trailed off, and he looked at Lyria. Her expression was somewhere between sad and stricken. He took her hand in his and kissed it softly. "Hey, beautiful, don't worry. I'm fine now. I'm getting my bearings, and maybe you're right. Maybe I need to rethink what I want. But I don't think I should make any quick decisions. Then again," he pulled her toward him and kissed her lips, "I made a pretty quick decision about you and so far it's turned out rather wonderfully, hasn't it?"

"Yes, it has," she said, but he noticed her smile didn't reach her eyes and she didn't say anything else.

"You said this was your first extended stay on the Jersey Shore," he said, changing the subject.

"It is."

"Well, we did the diner last night, but have you had some of our famous Boardwalk cuisine. Frozen custard? Or deep-fried Oreos?"

"I did have Sicilian pizza, but as for those others, no, I haven't tried them."

"Well, I know we've just eaten but you have to sample the treats we're known for. Let's take walk," Drew said as they put the rest of the dishes in the sink. "What about the arcades? Have you played skeeball yet?"

"Nope, can't say I have, although I've seen the signs for it."

"You haven't completely enjoyed the Shore until you've played a few rounds of skeeball, but I warn you in advance, it's addictive."

"I think I can control myself," she said.

She was wrong. Drew could see after the first game how much she enjoyed it, and by the third it was clear they were going to be there for a while. She picked up the game quickly, not that it was difficult, but her natural grace certainly helped as she rolled the ball straight down the aisle. He liked to play to see how many 100's he could hit in a game, which meant sometimes his score was great, sometimes lousy. Lyria, on the other hand, focused on consistency and hitting the center circles with 40 or 50 points. In the end, when they totaled up their tickets, his riskier approach yielded only a few more tickets than her conservative one. It made him wonder if there was a lesson for him there.

"What do we do with these?" she asked about the pile of tickets they'd accumulated.

"We can turn them in for prizes, but I have to warn you, the selection is generally disappointing and silly."

They walked over to the booth to make the exchange and Lyria smiled and nodded. "I see what you mean. This would be a lot of work for little reward. Good thing the game itself is so much fun."

A group of four kids was also at the booth, arguing and doing math as fast as they could to figure out what their best choices would be. They were trying to determine whether one big prize or several smaller prizes would be better, but there was clearly no agreement happening any time soon.

"Excuse me," Lyria said to the boy who looked the oldest. "I'm not planning to use my tickets. If I give them to you, will you make certain everyone gets some so they can get a better prize?"

"Are you sure?"

"Absolutely."

"Then I will. Thank you, miss," he said, showing a smile with missing teeth.

Drew's heart warmed at her action. He remembered how much these prizes meant when he was a kid and how he would save all summer for something which almost always broke too soon, after which his father would remind him that only things you truly worked for lasted. Her gift would matter to them. "You can add mine to those, too, but do your best to be fair."

"Yes, sir, thank you too." His reply could barely be heard over the squealing kids. Drew took her hand in his and kissed it as they walked back out into the sun. Lyria stopped as something tugged her dress.

"Are you a fairy?" a small voice said.

They turned to see the littlest of the children, a girl, standing behind them. "No, sweetness, I'm not."

"You look like one. I told my brother back there you're the prettiest lady I've ever seen. You could be a princess."

Lyria reached out and touched the girl's cheek, caressing it for a second before bending at the knees to look the girl in the eyes. Drew thought he felt her hand get warmer, but passed it off as Lyria reacting to the compliment. "What's your name?"

"Madeline."

"Well, Madeline, thank you. That's one of the nicest things anyone has ever said to me."

"You're welcome," came the quiet reply. The girl seemed mesmerized by Lyria. "You're quite lovely too, Madeline."

"I'm too small."

"Oh no, not at all." I see you growing into a

beautiful and smart woman. Now, don't stay away from your brother too long. You don't want him to worry about you wandering off."

"Okay. Goodbye, princess lady."

"Goodbye, angel."

As they walked away, Drew said, "I think you made that little girl's day."

"You may be right," she said, linking her arm on his.

* * *

Drew didn't know how right he was. The moment she placed a hand on the little girl, and once she was told her name, Lyria could connect with her body. She immediately learned Madeline suffered from terrible food allergies which limited her nutrition and her life. She'd never picked up a reading off someone so quickly and thought it must be because humans don't mask things as much as merfolk do and children are even more open. Fortunately, they were also easier to heal and with her brief touch, Lyria knew she'd made a difference to the girl's future.

It was the first time in years she healed someone without it being asked, demanded, or begged of her. She did it because she wanted to and because she could. It felt wonderful. She remembered her grandmother, the last woman to wear Melusine's Band, speaking with joy about some of her patients and what she was able to do for them. It was not something Lyria had experienced. Until now.

She was still feeling giddy when she asked if they could stop for lunch. "I'm hungry. What looks good to you?" she asked.

"You do," he said with a smile and a kiss.

"I meant to eat."

"So did I."

She kissed him fully, enjoying his playfulness. He showed this side so rarely and it pleased her to give him occasions to experience it. "What do you think I should try?" He wiggled his eyebrows. "That's available to purchase. On the Boardwalk."

"Ah, in that case, I think we should skip anything which could possibly be counted as nutritious, since we can order those at The Siren, and focus entirely on dessert and maybe some fried foods. Or fried desserts. We've got those too."

"Sounds good to me," she said."

It tasted even better. They bought zeppoles covered in powdered sugar, shared ice cream sandwiched between freshly made waffles, fried Oreos, and salt water taffy. The treats were sweet, sticky, and decidedly unhealthy. She couldn't remember when she'd had so much fun trying new foods. There certainly wasn't anything like this where she came from. She would miss it when she left. Even the feeling of being stuffed.

As the thought occurred to her, she stopped it. Missing things was part of her life; she should be used to it. She missed her freedom, knowing what her day would hold, being able to *decide* what her day would hold, and long periods of uninterrupted time. Her world was about duty and responsibility. She could be called to help at a moment's notice no matter what she was doing. She should be used to giving things up, especially pleasurable things.

Not liking her bitter thoughts, Lyria cleared her

head to stay in the moment. She wanted to focus on Drew and what they were doing. Nothing more. He kissed her unexpectedly, which helped to bring her back. They ate, walked, and ate again. She loved watching the enjoyment on the faces of the other visitors as they received their choices and took their first bite.

"You're smiling," Drew said.

"Shouldn't I be?"

"Definitely, but since I haven't done or said anything endearing in the last few minutes, it can't be me, so I'm hurt." He put on a pout.

"Not going to work, sorry. I have a younger cousin I grew up with and I'm immune to those looks."

He laughed. "Duly noted. So, what's making you smile?"

"Everything. I am having a wonderful time, the sun is shining, and I'm with you." She took a spoonful of her frozen custard which was her favorite so far and enjoyed its cold sweetness. "Besides, you can't be sad while eating this stuff."

"I suppose you're right."

"Suppose? This was your idea."

"I know, and I love seeing you enjoy it, but I grew up here. It's not quite as wonderful from my perspective. What I tend to see are how run down the businesses look and which ones are gone. In the crowds of tourists I see the people we love for the money they spend and hate for the way they tend to treat our properties and the locals."

"Sounds like a difficult balance for the community."

"It can be."

"Speaking of balance, is that safe?" she said

pointing to a metal monstrosity with small cars racing around and people screaming.

"The Wild Mouse ride? Of course. We're very careful about our roller coasters here. Haven't you ever been on one?"

She'd never even seen one. "No. It looks dangerous. Is it exciting or scary? I can't tell."

"That's part of the fun. It's both. Do you want to try it?"

She wasn't certain. It looked risky, but the sense she was getting from the people as they stepped off was one of exhilaration. "Will you come with me?"

"Absolutely. I love roller coasters. Come on."

He bought their tickets and as they waited, he stood behind her and put his arms around her waist. It was comfortable and reassuring, which was good, because the closer they got to the front of the line, the more nervous she became. By the time they were seated she was shaking.

He put his hand over hers. "Try to relax and if you feel like screaming—go for it. I always do."

So did she. There was no way not to when the car plunged toward the ground at what felt like a harrowing speed. Over and over she was lifted and dropped, and when they got off, her throat was sore. Screaming was another rarity among merfolk. It didn't work well under water. But her heart was beating fast and she felt completely aware and alive.

"That was—amazing. I'm all tingly and jumpy."

"Yup, that's the result of a good coaster ride. It wakes you up. I guess it's the relief of getting off safely after fearing for your life for a few minutes."

"I suppose," she said, although she didn't like the

reminder of fearing for her life since this was the reason she came here in the first place. When it was real, there was nothing exhilarating about it.

They walked further along the boardwalk than Lyria had on her own and as she leaned against him, she was surprised by a familiar image. "What's that?" she asked, pointing to the green logo over a shop.

"You're looking at the commercialization of the boardwalk. Some people just can't do without their favorite brand of coffee no matter where they are or how expensive it is."

"They use a mermaid to sell coffee?"

"What mermaid?"

"Don't you see the mermaid in the circle, with the long hair and crown and star on her head?"

"That's a mermaid?"

"Yes, with her split tail on either side of her."

"I've never heard of a mermaid with two tails."

"Then you don't know the story of Melusine," she said.

"You're right, I don't. But since you've clearly never had Starbucks, which I think is even stranger, I'll make an exception this once and we'll go in to someplace that's part of a chain. You can try one of the most popular coffees in the country, and I can learn about Melusine."

A few minutes later they sat at a small table sharing something called a Rice Krispy Treat and Lyria tasted the joys of her first vanilla latte, which Drew insisted required cinnamon on the top. It was sweet and strong. "I can certainly understand why people like this place. This is wonderful," she said as she licked the foam from her lips.

"Do that again and I'm going to need to find a private location for us." She couldn't help but giggle although she could tell the hunger in his eyes was real. "So tell me about this two-finned mermaid."

Lyria took another sip of her drink. She needed to explain it as a story, not her family history. She thought for a moment then began. "The story has been told in many ways and assigned to many cultures, but this is how I know it. Melusine, the daughter of a powerful and magical king, married a human whom she thought she could trust with her heart. He told her, of course, that he loved her and would gladly be by her side always."

"Oh, this never turns out well," Drew said. "Go on."

"He knew from the beginning she was a mermaid, which is different from many of the tales, but when she bore him daughters and not sons he turned against her and locked her away until she could produce an heir for him. He was king now and she would do as he said. While in isolation, she learned that her husband only married her for her magic and power and didn't love her at all. She decided to take her revenge and protect her daughters as best she could. She took back the magical amulet she'd given him, which allowed him to live in both the human and mermaid world, destroying him—and herself—in the process."

"She killed him?"

"Yes."

"Harsh, but sounds like he deserved it."

"It was a long time before mermaids in Melusine's line came near humans again. Or so it's said," she hastened to add.

"Duplicitous asshole. I know what it's like

dealing with people like that. Although I can't say I've ever been married to one, so that's good."

Lyria took a sip of her drink and didn't say anything. She was the one who was duplicitous in this relationship and she didn't like thinking about it. Still, she reasoned, there was no reason for her to tell him her truths. She didn't need his trust, even though his words, the sentiment, made her uncomfortable. He thought she was trustworthy. Of course she was. She was only keeping knowledge of her species and the danger she was in from him. It wasn't as if that had ever gotten her kind in trouble before.

She reminded herself she was leaving in a few days. He would never need to know.

"Still," he said, breaking into her thoughts, "offering trust is no guarantee of anything. People lie. In my case, trust didn't help at all."

"With your business partner and friend?"

"Yup, I'm here because I believed someone foolishly.

"There's more to your tale then you've told me."

"Yes, only mine's not a fable."

Neither is mine, she thought. "Will you tell me the whole story?"

* * *

Drew didn't understand how the conversation circled around to this topic again. Clearly it was on his mind. He supposed it was because talking to Lyria was like confiding to someone on a plane. It gave you release without any concern. With her leaving in a few days, she couldn't use anything he said against him. Also, with his experience having fun at The Siren the last two days everything felt murky again. Not that it was particularly clear before, but it was decidedly worse now. "If you'd come to visit at the beginning of the year, we wouldn't have met. I was living in Chicago where I'd been since college and business school."

"What did you do?"

"Mostly management consulting and new product launches for midsize companies. We helped them gain market shares and generate buzz."

"Did you like it?"

"I did then. It was exciting and fun to help our clients. Not to mention the fact it made me a lot of money, which was very important."

"Why?"

The question made him stop. No one had ever asked before. He thought before answering, "Money was always a problem in my house growing up. It was the reason we couldn't do things or have things. Other people having money either caused arguments because, I think, my dad felt threatened or had tirades around how rich people were corrupt and liars. Those usually happened when my dad was between jobs."

"What did he do?"

"He's a contractor with his own business most of the time. Sometimes he had to work for other people when things got slow."

"I'm guessing from your tone he didn't like that."

"No, he preferred to be independent. I wanted the same thing, but I also wanted wealth and class. He wanted both his sons to go into the family business."

"The other son, this is the older brother you mentioned earlier?"

141

"Yes, Michael. He's always done everything my father wanted. I'm not sure the guy's ever had a thought of his own." She didn't say anything and he heard the coldness of his words in the silence. "Sorry, I didn't intend to be so nasty. Michael and I are very different and we've always wanted different things, but for some reason I can't quite begin to fathom, I've always felt competitive with him. Of course, seeing him with my high school girlfriend a few days ago didn't help."

"Ouch. That couldn't have been fun."

"Not at all," he said, although thinking about it now didn't bother him. Having Lyria around was definitely helping.

"I told you I have a cousin. We're the same way. Very different, often arguing, but mostly we're very close. I can always count on her. I love her and she loves me."

"I guess Michael and I care about each other. We don't talk often."

"Not even now that you're home?"

"I'm back. I'm not home. And no, especially not now. I'm sure my family thinks I deserved what happened to me."

"What did happen?"

"After a few years working for other companies and learning what I thought I needed, I started my business with a loan from Mr. V. and a friend from business school. Things were slow and difficult in the beginning, but after the first two years we were doing well, very well. I paid Mr. V. back, with interest and visited with my father to show off my shiny new car, the one I still have, and my expensive watch. Not my finest moment, I can now admit, but damn it felt good in the moment. Our client list—and our bank accounts—were growing steadily.

"As I mentioned earlier, my so-called friend sold me out. We were doing a project for a company and without my knowing it, he was working for a competing company and selling them our clients' secrets. Once they had what they needed, they gave him a job and I got the shaft. When the word got out, every client bailed. They didn't care that I had nothing to do with what happened. I was guilty by association and couldn't be trusted. I was lucky I didn't get jail time."

"That's awful," she said.

"Within weeks I was left with nothing but a ruined reputation a possible lawsuit which I settled, and no clue how to fix the situation."

"And you lost a friend."

He nodded. "I did. We'd been through a lot together both in school and after. We'd lived on packaged noodles and energy drinks, and slept in the office as often as we did at home for the first two years. I thought I knew him. I never imagined he could turn on me and destroy what we built."

"Why did he do it?"

Shrugging, he said, "I have no idea. When he told me what he'd done, I sat there, stunned. I remember he said it was nothing personal. He was offered a deal he didn't want to pass up. I still don't understand how it wasn't personal. I put everything into that business. That made it very personal"

"I'm so sorry, Drew," she said.

She took his hand in hers. It was the first time

he'd let anyone comfort him about what happened. Up until then he'd been happy to hold on to his anger. He'd avoided talking about it whenever possible, which wasn't difficult since he wasn't close to anyone here. But after this conversation, he began to feel the grief. It wasn't comfortable, but it wasn't as horrible as he expected. "I never imagined I could be so low."

"How did you end up coming ho—back."

He smiled as she repeated his word to him. "It was Mr. V. to the rescue again, although this time it wasn't me needing him to help, it was the other way around. He went into an assisted living facility not long ago, and his doctor told him he needed to slow down. Ever since Nico was killed, he's thrown himself into running The Siren. He called me a few weeks after my fiasco to say he'd had a fall. He didn't break a hip, but it was a near thing and the doctor ordered him off his feet. He asked if I would run the place while he took a leave and regained his strength." Drew laughed. "He stops by once in a while to make sure I'm doing things right, but otherwise he lets me manage as I want. I worked there when I was in high school. Sometimes it's weird to be the manager."

"And sometimes it's fun," she said. He raised an eyebrow. "You had fun last night, admit it," she said.

He couldn't. He appreciated her attempts, but it didn't matter if she was right. He wasn't ready to look to closely at how great his shift went the evening before. Cooking for tourists was not how he wanted to spend his time or earn his income. This was a temporary situation done to help out an old friend. "Come on, let's walk back. By the time we get back to the apartment, we'll be hungry again."

She agreed and picked up her empty cup and the plate, but the look she gave him suggested the topic wasn't closed.

As they walked back the sun was setting, the day cooling. Lyria walked to the rail at the edge of the boardwalk where the sand began, took a deep breath, and sighed. "I love the smells here."

"Old fry oil and dead fish?"

She gave him a funny look. "Sugar and salt. Sugar from all the sweets and the salt of the ocean. I know you're jaded and grew up with all of this, but it's new to me."

"Well, don't tell anyone, but spending the day with you has been more fun than I've had here in years."

"I'm glad, and I won't tell." She turned and kissed him. What he thought was going to be quick became a much deeper embrace, as she put her hands to his face and pulled him close. He breathed in her sweet scent and put his arms around her. Her tongue explored his mouth and he couldn't stop thinking of all the things she'd done with that tongue, all he'd done to her. Her natural passion was a turn-on, and he wished they were closer to The Siren so he could have her naked beneath him.

Of course, he remembered, stroking his hand over her ass and feeling nothing beneath, she was pretty naked already. He didn't think he would ever understand her aversion to underwear. He would also never complain about it. It was exciting to know with a few quick moves she would be completely bare, available to his touch.

He moved his mouth to her jaw, kissed his way

145

up to her ear, and said, "I am not going to be able to walk any further for a few minutes."

"Perhaps we need to move to a bench and sit for a little while."

"Definitely."

Fortunately, there were benches every few steps and it was easy to find a vacant one. "Guess this means I shouldn't keep kissing you," she said as she leaned against him.

"Not for a little while," he said.

"Too bad. I like exciting you."

"I like it too, but there are a lot of people around. And families."

"Good point," she said. "I'll behave."

"Which is not something I'll normally encourage you to do."

She smiled and kissed him softly. "Good to know."

As they sat in silence, Drew became aware he was calm for the first time in months. Unfortunately, as soon as he thought it, his mind began racing will all the reasons he shouldn't be calm, all the things he needed to be focused on to get back on track. Nothing could have cooled his erection faster.

"I'm ready." He knew he sounded harsh, but he couldn't help it. "Let's head back to The Siren. I'm sure there are a ton of things needing my attention since I've been away for so long."

"It's only been a few hours," she said.

"That's all it takes."

She looked as though she were going to say something else, but instead she stood, took his hand and they walked back.

* * *

"Tonight is the full moon. This is unacceptable. You assured me we'd have her by now," Fiero said. The deadline was coming up fast and he was no closer to having what he wanted. What he needed. The rage inside him was building.

"I said nothing of the sort," said the merman. "I said with me on your side, you'd have her sooner than you would without me."

"Yes, which is the reason I didn't kill you, Wilmar."

"I also offered to help you to avoid detection by her family, which I have. Her family has not been able to trace you or keep you from your search."

"Which has thus far yielded no results," he yelled.

"I am aware of this, my lord."

Fiero liked the sound of "my lord" coming from one of the merfolk, although he did not think for a moment this one was sincere. He knew better than to trust someone who was out for revenge, and the male clearly had something against Lyria and her family, otherwise he would not have sought out Fiero. Still, as long as he was useful, Fiero would keep him around. Once he was of no further use—well, that was a pleasure for another time.

Fiero was looking forward to having his revenge over all the mercreatures. When merfolk had turned their back on Fiero's mother after she came home and told them she was pregnant by a kelpie and needed shelter they made a dangerous enemy. To them, mixing the blood of those two races was an

147

abomination. *He* was an abomination. For the way they had treated his mother and him, he would see to it those who hurt an innocent woman and her unborn child paid for their shallowness and shortsightedness.

He needed all three bracelets to rule the seas. Separately they were powerful. Once he brought them together to recreate Melusine's bracelet they would make him unstoppable.

Wilmar interrupted his thoughts. "There is something you haven't tried, my lord."

The fool was trying what little remaining patience Fiero had, and his race was not known for having any patience at all. "And what might that be?"

"I know of a place she liked to visit on occasion."

"And you chose not to share this with me sooner?"

"Truly, I thought the blood potion made from her injury would be all you needed to locate her."

Very little the wiry creature said was likely true, unless it served him in some way. But since they both wanted Lyria, there was no reason to think his words were a lie. "How do you come by this information?"

"From following her."

"Tell me," Fiero said and watched for the man's reaction. It was likely the merman would hide more than he expressed, but the Sea Dragon was as good at reading expressions and body language as any sea creature who has to communicate by both visual and auditory means.

Sure enough there was a pause before he answered. "During our relationship she had a tendency to disappear every now and then, so I decided to follow her to see where she went."

Fiero knew he'd learn there was more to the man's story than simply wanting to be on the winning side, as he had claimed. Jilted lovers always had a score to settle. Matters of the heart always weakened a man. This was another reason why an arranged marriage would be additionally beneficial. "Thought she might be cheating on you?"

"Of course not," he said. Fiero looked at the merman and said nothing, enjoying the confirmation of the man's arrogance. He didn't know or care much about what made a merman attractive to a female, but he very much doubted it was this one's looks that held a woman for long. There was a coldness in his eyes. Fiero recognized it as one he saw every day in his own reflection. The man had a very high opinion of himself, but it was unlikely it was shared by others. Fortunately, it was a tool to be used against him and Fiero believed in using everything and anyone he was given. "Then what?"

"Simply because I knew she wasn't cheating, didn't mean I wanted her going off… unsupervised."

"You followed her. What did you discover?"

"On several occasion she visited various points on the northeast coast of North America."

"Colder waters up there."

"Not something ocean creatures generally care about."

"Colder air as well." When it came to being out of the water, most aquatic shifters preferred warm air in their lungs and on their skin.

"True, but Lyria isn't a particularly warm female."

"I will take your word on that," Fiero said.

"As you should. Once you do find her, she will not easily do your bidding." The merman continued with a laugh. "Are you really willing to fight with your bedmate?"

Fiero didn't take well to being thought a fool, and before the male could take another breath he was being looked down on by a fully grown dragon who, with claws sharper than the spear-like bill of a marlin, could sever a head from its shoulders with a casual wave of his hand. In this form he used telepathic communication. *What makes you think I will permit a fight?*

The merman bowed and took a step back. Fiero knew it was as much out of fear than respect, but either would do for the time being. He did ultimately want respect. Ruling for any length of time based on fear was exhausting and he intended to have a long rule. As he shifted back into human form, he wondered what it would be like to have a true queen at his side. Someone who understood him.

He shook his head at the foolish thought. Clearly his mother's warm heart still influenced him. He would have to be cautious in the future.

"Is something wrong, my lord?"

Fiero also needed to school his features better. "Yes. Neither the female nor the stone are in my possession and time is running out. We need to find her and fast, because you don't want my wrath focused on you."

"Of course not. We will dispatch the naiads to the Atlantic coast. There is still enough of the blood potion for them to use to track her. I am certain she will be yours soon. And once we locate her, sir, this will ensure she comes with you without a fight." Wilmar pulled out an agate necklace and let it dangle from between his fingers.

Fiero gave a small dangerous smile. He directed his fury at Wilmar "Not what you'd promised you'd bring me back from that little venture, but it is something. Lyria had better be mine soon or you will wish you were born a single-celled organism when I am through with you."

Chapter Seven

Sunday, One day past the full moon

Saturday night was longer and more exhausting than Friday, and after another late-night swim, Lyria and Drew showered off the salt, even though she didn't need and collapsed in bed. When she awoke and stretched in the morning, she realized it was the first day her injury didn't hurt. Looking down at her hip, she saw the red line had faded significantly. She sent up a prayer of thanks to the goddess for her body's progress. Magically induced injuries had unpredictable healing times, and she was relieved that the pain was gone. Looking next to her, she also realized it was the first morning she woke before Drew.

Deciding to take advantage of her discovery, Lyria made a quick trip to the bathroom, rinsed her mouth, then returned, taking a condom out of Drew's nightstand. He was on his back and already bare to the waist, the covers having been pulled down. She gently stroked his chest with her hand and watched as the thin blanket moved in response to his cock hardening. Merman and human males shared this tendency to wake somewhat if not fully aroused. With previous lovers she often found it annoying, especially if she wanted to sleep in. It was part of the reason she rarely spent the night with a male. Today, however, it was exactly what she wanted.

Gently pulling the covers off the rest of the way, she caressed his legs from his knees up to his inner thighs. He was so damn sexy she could almost be happy simply touching him and watching as her actions filtered their way into his dreams.

Almost.

She wanted more than gentle touches. She was hungry for him and could feel her body becoming wet and ready. Leaning in, she gently licked the length of his cock, pulling back the foreskin to reveal the sensitive tip. She ran her tongue around the head and was rewarded with a surge of stiffness followed by a drop of moisture. Hoping she didn't wake him, she gently rolled the condom down his length before straddling him. She positioned his cock at her entrance, then sank down on him, taking him deep within her. Leaning forward, she kissed him as she rocked her hips. His eyes opened slowly, then, as though sensing everything at once, opened completely.

"You really are a man's fantasy come true," he said and pulled her into a deep kiss as he lifted his hips to get further into her.

"Am I?"

"To be woken by a beautiful woman who is already in the process of having sex with you? You're better than a fantasy, because I couldn't ever have imagined this would actually happen."

His words alone made her tingle, and she brought them together with a kiss. He wrapped his arms around her as they moved together. In this position he wasn't as deep, but she loved being close. They continued to kiss and touch each other, awakening in a different way. Lyria was so happy in the moment she wished her magic included the ability to stop or slow time.

With his hands on her shoulders, Drew pushed her back into a sitting position. "Now this is a view I could get used to." He reached for her breasts, playing with the nipples until they hardened, then pinching them lightly until she gasped and arched her back.

"Yes, beauty, offer yourself to me."

She put her palms on his chest and lifted slowly off his cock before coming down in a controlled motion. His moan was worth her restraint, as challenging as it was.

She continued to move as slowly until he grabbed her hips and forced her to meet his thrust.

"I'll take that as a hint," she said and together they moved in an increasingly rapid rhythm, their pleasure building along with their need. When he reached between them to tease her clitoris, she pushed herself into his finger, taking his cock deeply into her body and sending both of them spiraling toward a climax.

"Don't stop," Lyria gasped. "Please don't stop."

"I won't," he said, sounding as breathless as she did.

From there on, nothing beyond "yes" and "oh God" were intelligible between moans, and moments later her orgasm approached.

"I'm, I'm..." she tried.

"I know."

The pleasure crashed and coursed through her like

a thunderstorm and she bit her lip to keep from screaming. Drew followed closely behind, thrusting even deeper inside her, lifting her when his ass came off the bed. She tightened herself around him, increasing both their pleasure until she wasn't able to stay upright, and she collapsed, boneless, on top of him.

They lay together for several minutes as she enjoyed the rapid beat of his heart, the warmth of his body against hers.

"Now that's the way to wake up. Even better than coffee," he said.

"Knowing how much you like your coffee, I'm taking that as a compliment."

He turned her face toward him so he could kiss her. It started gently, then became passionate. She wrapped her arms around him and surrendered to the pleasure of his touch, his hunger.

She wished they could spend the day in bed, but less than an hour later they were getting the restaurant ready for the day's customers. There was no way to explain to the other servers how much Lyria loved working at The Siren. For most of them it was a way to earn money for fun or to save for something important, like a car. To her it was a glorious change from the heavy responsibility of healer. Back in her world, on the occasions when she was called to help someone in dire need, she never knew in advance if her skills would be enough or if Fate had other plans. It was not her decision to make. She was there only to give her best and hope, along with the loved ones, that it would be enough. Every time it wasn't, part of her died too. The thought of the decades to come was both terrifying and exhausting.

Waiting on tables, on the other hand, was wonderful and predictable. Guests almost always arrived in a good mood, looking forward to time out. If they had something in mind, you brought it to them, or there were specials you could suggest if they wanted to try something new. Lyria didn't even mind if a customer was difficult or complained. There was always something else you could offer, a way to make things right. When their meal did go smoothly, their pleasure was obvious. Then the next diners arrived and the process started all over. She smiled at the people at her tables, and most of the time they smiled back. They didn't fear her or worry she couldn't do her job. They placed their orders, then generally ignored her.

Lyria checked herself in the mirror before heading out to the floor, marveling at her uniform. She wore a light blue polo shirt with the Siren name and logo embroidered on it and a short skirt made out of something called denim which Jody had given her. The clothes were heavy on her body, but she liked fitting in with the others. Even wearing shoes wasn't the hardship it started out to be.

On Sundays The Siren was only open from 11:00 until 4:00 and served something Drew called brunch, which he explained was a combination of breakfast and lunch together. She thought it sounded like a fun idea. When she saw the mix of food on the menu, she understood the appeal. Typical human breakfast foods and sides were mixed with the heavier choices of later in the day, creating something completely different. She wondered if she could learn to make some of it herself. She was definitely going to miss the food here when she left.

She bobbled the water glass she was filling when the thought hit her. Fortunately, she wasn't pouring over the table.

She didn't want to miss anything. Or anyone.

But after nearly four days it was already impossible.

She was still tingling from the sex she'd enjoyed that morning with Drew, who was one of the hottest and most caring men she'd ever met. She liked the staff at The Siren. Jody, Joe, and Neil were warm people with whom she enjoyed spending time. They talked before and after their shifts, and she looked forward to seeing them when she came in each day.

Having familiar faces, people to count on, was so different for her. She'd never realized how pleasant it could be, or how much she would enjoy it. For a second she wondered if she could find a way to visit after she was free of Fiero's demands, but that was nothing more than wishful thinking. Her time here had to end, and there was nothing she could do to stop it. But she was going to take her new knowledge with her and when she returned home, she would start accepting and creating friendships beyond her cousin.

While she was enjoying this vacation from her real life, she found it interesting to watch Drew struggle with responsibilities and a life he claimed he didn't want. It was frighteningly familiar and she couldn't help but wonder if she appeared as distracted and confused to Amina. Being with Drew made her see it was important to be happy and find joy where you were, and not spend energy trying to run from what couldn't be changed. It was something she would need to remember once she returned.

Assuming everything turned out well and she didn't end up the married prisoner of the Sea Dragon. Or dead. Hard to know which was worse.

Looking at the moon, one day past full, and visible even in the sunlit sky, Lyria knew it wasn't going to be easy to say goodbye to Drew and her time here. Being free of her usual responsibilities not only allowed her to enjoy being on land and with a human, but allowed her to see how limited she'd allowed her life to be. How she held back on opportunities for joy and fun.

It wasn't a pretty picture. She promised herself she'd ask Amina for help. She was ready to make a change.

She'd spent too large a part of the last 15 years whining and bemoaning her position, seeing her lot as an unearned punishment instead of as the gift and opportunity it was. This was what her grandmother tried to explain to her. She'd ignored it.

With any luck, before she needed to leave she'd be able to open Drew's eyes to the wonder and happiness available to him. She couldn't imagine giving him a better gift, after all he'd shown her.

Even after she left him, and she must, she would be different and it didn't matter if she didn't wish to be. He'd shown her the true power of connection between a male and female, and she accepted she would no longer be satisfied without it. She wasn't certain it was a happy revelation, but she'd never been one to ignore the truth. It bothered her somewhat that she hadn't been able to completely shield her heart. Even after all she knew to be true, the knowledge of Melusine's ugly fate didn't protect her. She was going to have to be careful in the future.

Lyria shook her head to clear it as her first customer of the day, a distinguished man using a cane was seated at her favorite table, one with the best view in the restaurant. She brought over a glass of ice water and pot of coffee, placed the glass on the table and said, "Welcome to The Siren. I'm Lyria. Would you like some coffee?"

"Yes, thank you. You're new here."

"I am," she said. "You must come here often."

"I practically lived here at one point." He held out a hand and said, "I'm Angelo Vardini, the owner."

"Oh my, Mr. Vardini. I'm so sorry. I hope my not knowing who you were isn't a problem."

He put a hand over the one he already held. "Not at all, my dear. I was simply noticing the beautiful new server Drew has hired to take care of me and our customers."

"Thank you. Let me pour your coffee. Do you want to hear about our specials?"

"No, surprise me. Tell Drew I'm here and not only would I like to see him, but he should send out whatever is his favorite thing to make." Clearly he'd heard Drew had taken over the kitchen.

"I can tell you right now, sir, it's something called Eggs Benedict." Drew had made some before her shift started and once she tasted it, she cleared her plate in no time. "It looks odd and rather messy, but it tastes fabulous."

"I'm familiar with the dish. You're not from around here."

It was a statement. Apparently explaining what Eggs Benedict were gave her away somehow. "No, sir. I only came up here recently."

159

"Well, I hope you're enjoying yourself and Drew is taking good care of you."

"Excuse me?" She wondered if this man could tell she was involved with Drew.

"As an employer, my dear, but given how flustered you are, I'm guessing there is something else going on."

It was upsetting to know she was not hiding her emotions well from a human, something which should have come automatically to her. "I'll let Drew know you're here and put your order in. Would you like anything else, sir?"

"Not at the moment other than you calling me Angelo. Everyone does except Drew, and that's because he was so young when we met."

She managed a smile. He was easy to like. "Angelo it is. I'll be right back." She headed to the kitchen before she let anything else slip to the observant older man. She didn't see Drew at first, and, assuming he was in another part of the kitchen, she wrote her order and placed it where Neil and Jody would see it.

A cold kiss on the back of her neck made her jump and squeal. "Did I startle you?" Drew said, putting his arms around her from behind.

"Yes, and your lips are freezing."

"Sorry, was getting things organized in the walk-in. Must have been in there longer than I thought."

She turned to face him. "I'm sure I can find a way to warm you up."

"I have no doubt, beautiful. You did a wonderful job this morning." He kissed her again, this time long enough for the cold to leave his embrace. Once the orders started coming in and he was working, he would be hot and sweaty in no time. The thought sent a shiver completely unrelated to cold through her body. "I like it when you react to my kisses that way," he said.

"I like it when you kiss me that way." As he leaned toward her, she pulled back a bit. "First customers are arriving. We'd better not start something."

"Drat," he said with a pout and she laughed at the silly expression. "I hate it when you're right."

"You may be happier when I tell you one of them is Angelo Vardini. He's seated at one of my tables by the window."

"Mr. V. is here? Nice!" With a smile on his face, he let her go and left the kitchen at a fast clip. Clearly the man was important to him and Lyria liked seeing the happy expression on his face. She was especially glad it was happening more frequently.

She dreaded what would happen to his smile if she ever needed to tell him the truth about who she was. His trust had been so recently betrayed by someone he cared about. She hoped that would never happen because of her.

* * *

"Mr. V., what a great surprise. You should have told me you were coming."

"Why should I do that? It's my restaurant, and you know I like dropping in suddenly to see how you're doing."

"I do," Drew said. Mr. V. arrived unannounced a week after Drew started managing the place, and he found Drew practically buried under piles of orders and phone messages. It hadn't been his best moment, and he worried Mr. V. would regret his decision, but the man smiled his calming smile, sat himself beside Drew, and with the same patience he'd shown when Drew was a sophomore, helped him to make sense of everything and get things in an order which made sense for him.

"So who's the beautiful new girl who took my order?"

"Lyria? Oh, she's not new." Mr. V. raised an eyebrow. "I mean she is, but she's not someone I hired. I'm mean she's working here, but she's…" He didn't know how to finish the sentence.

"She's what, boy?"

"I don't know, actually. She's waiting tables because I pulled Jody into the kitchen after Stanley and Todd left."

"I heard the rumor." Drew wasn't surprised. Mr. V. knew everything about his place.

"Well, one no-showed and has never been back, and the other walked out during a shift. I think that qualifies as quitting."

"Why didn't I hear this from you?" He put up a hand to stop whatever answer Drew was considering. "Let's start this from the beginning, please."

"It only happened Friday night," Drew said and he explained the drama of the past two days and how he and Jody were managing.

"How does your Lyria fit in to all of this?"

"What do you mean?"

"You said you didn't hire her, but unless I'm losing my mind, which I'm not, she took my order a

162

few minutes ago." Drew rubbed his hands across his forehead. "Oh, I recognize that motion. You've gotten yourself into something you didn't expect and aren't certain how to handle."

Drew had foolishly forgotten how observant the man was, and how well he knew him. "That's an understatement. I saw Lyria for the first time Wednesday when she came in during jazz night and we clicked."

"Clicked?" Mr. V. said.

"Please don't ask me to be more specific." He was not giving details about his love life to Mr. V.

"Okay, go on."

"There isn't much to tell. She disappeared after we…clicked, then came back the next day. We've been together pretty much nonstop since. She was with me Friday night when the guys walked out and jumped in to help."

"That was nice of her."

"It was, is. She's great. Supportive, a wonderful listener and great in the—" He stopped. Damn. "She's a terrific kisser."

"We'll leave it at that. So what's the problem?"

"It's not exactly a problem."

"Spit it out, boy."

"I've only known her for a little over three days but it seems like much longer. Hell, I just realized she's never told me her last name. She's supposed to be leaving in a few days and the thought of it ties me in knots, which is crazy."

"Why is it crazy?"

"Three days, Mr. V.? There's no reason for me to be feeling this way, not to mention the fact I don't know

163

what the hell I'll be doing or where I'll be living in a few months, so getting close to someone is a stupid idea."

Mr. V. took a slow sip of his coffee. "Leaving the second part aside, I knew my Cecilia for a week before I proposed and it was hell to wait even that long because I knew I was going to ask her to marry me after our first date."

"Really?"

"Absolutely. People said we were nuts, of course. We were too young, we barely knew each other, we had no money. It was all true, but the bigger truth was—we knew. Of course, we still needed to wait a few months because Cici was the oldest daughter and first to marry and in her family, this meant a big lavish Catholic wedding. Can't plan those overnight," he said with a smile of remembrance. "Longest months of my life, but never once did I doubt we were doing the right thing."

"Did she?"

"Not as far as I know. We had our problems, our fights, times without money, and our toughest period when we learned Nico would be our only child, but we always had each other. Our commitment never wavered even if our emotions did or the situation were hellish. There was no one else I wanted by my side once I met her."

"So, I'm not crazy to be feeling this way about Lyria?"

"Oh, you're completely insane, my boy, but it doesn't make you wrong." Drew smiled but continued to rub his hand over his forehead. "Is there something else troubling you?"

"Our conversation is reminding me that tomorrow I have to put out an advertisement for two new chefs."

"Why?"

"What do you mean, why?"

"At most you only need one."

Drew saw where this was going. "No. No, no, no. This is not a career move for me, Mr. V. I'm here to help you until you can come back as manager, and that's fine, honestly. I'm glad I could be here. But once you're ready, I'm out. Two new folks in front of the range and things will be back on course."

"I apologize. I got the impression you enjoyed yourself these last few days."

"I have, but this is not what I want."

"You're sure?"

"Come on, Mr. V. You know me."

"Yes, I do."

"You've heard me talk for years about what I want and you know it's not a job like this. No offense."

"None taken, and what I know is you don't want to be anything like your father and that's always been more important to you than doing what you like."

"That's not true."

Mr. V. said nothing as he continued to drink his coffee.

"My decisions have nothing to do with him."

Mr. V. motioned for a refill.

"I've always wanted to do something more with my life."

"'More' is kind of vague, don't you think? More than what?"

"More than—" Drew stopped. The next word was going to be "him" and the reference to his father would only prove Mr. V. right. Was he?

"Drew, you have the smarts and the drive to do

165

and be whatever you choose, but I don't think you've been picturing a life based on your heart. It's all been on your head, what you think you should do to be as different, or better, than your dad. Things you've seen in magazines or in books or movies on what success is. Worse, I think you make a lot of your decisions because of that, which means you're building a life on a foundation of anger, not joy or love."

Now it was Drew's turn to be silent.

"You know, I wasn't much of a cook or much of a manager when I first took over this place, but I wanted to do something which let me be around people, hire people I thought deserved a chance, give back to this community, and whenever possible, work with my family. Cici was with me almost every day, and when she wasn't working, she stopped by. Nico's highchair was at this table for years. It was hard and sometimes hellish work, and there were times when we weren't certain how we were going to pay the bills but it was all based on love so no matter what, at the end of the day, I felt great. Can you say that about the work you've done?"

The answer was easy, but uncomfortable. "No."

"Do you want to?"

"Yes," he said.

Mr. V. reached out and took his hand. "Then start listening to your heart, my boy, before it's too late. Let go of the crap influencing it and, I think, holding you back. Be honest with yourself and find what you love, then find a way to do it. And if there's a roof over your head, food on the table, and someone to come home to at night, what else do you really need?"

This time Drew had no answer. His beautiful

166

apartment in Chicago, his sports car and name in the paper certainly hadn't helped when everything had gone to hell. Although he was glad at the time no one else was affected by what happened, sitting here with Mr. V., he could admit it would have been nice to have gone through it with someone instead of alone.

Drew saw Lyria coming over with Mr. V.'s order and decided he'd use it as his cue. "Are you going to stick around?"

"I may stay for a bit, see how things are running without me."

"Then I'd better get back to the kitchen. Talk to you later."

He didn't like the smile Mr. V. gave him and was fairly certain he wasn't getting away with anything. As usual.

* * *

"Here are your eggs, Angelo."

"Thanks, beautiful. Those do look good." She waited as he took a bite, putting all the flavors together. "Mmm, that boy has the touch."

"I agree, and I'm glad you like it. More coffee?"

"Only if you pour yourself a cup and join me."

"Thank you, but I can't. I have other tables."

Mr. V. motioned to the nearest waitress. "Doll, could you cover this girl's tables for the length of a cup of coffee?"

"Absolutely, Angelo. Take all the time you need, Lyria."

"Thanks," Lyria said. She filled a mug for herself and refilled Angelo's, passed the carafe off to another server, and sat down.

"So, why does a lovely young visitor decide to wait tables at a Jersey Shore dive on her vacation?"

"It's no dive, but you already know that."

"You didn't answer my question," he said.

"You are very direct."

"At my age, it's a virtue. Drew says you're leaving in two days, but he doesn't sound happy about it, and you don't look happy about it. So what can be done to change this?"

She sweetened and lightened then sipped her coffee to buy herself some time, although there wasn't much to consider. The answer was clear. "Nothing, I'm sorry to say."

"Nonsense. If a different result is what you want, then a different choice needs to be made."

"It's not so simple."

"You and Drew really are peas in a pod," he said.

"What do you mean?"

"You both know what you want, but for some reason, rather than finding a way to make it happen, you latch on to any and all excuses you can find to make sure it doesn't. What do you have against being happy?"

The question made her put down her cup midway to her mouth. She didn't think she had anything against happiness—only that it always seemed to be out of her reach. It was something for others but not for her, ever since her profession had been handed to her. She didn't have choices. Did she?

"I suppose the answers don't seem easy for either of you, but trust me when I say that they are easier than you think and will be worth it."

"You really believe that."

"Absolutely. When my son, Nico, died I expected to work here until I died. I figured I'd just drop dead in the kitchen one day. It was better than doing nothing and thinking all the time about what I'd lost. My days were routine, but busy. Then I read about Drew's business set back. Don't tell him, but once he moved out to Chicago I started getting the papers from out there. Anyway, once I heard, I knew the reason I hadn't sold the place a few years ago when I thought I had no one to give it to."

Lyria sat with his words for a moment until she understood. "You knew. You knew Drew lost everything, that he was struggling."

He nodded. "I've known him a long time. Do you know how we met?"

She was curious about Angelo's perspective on the meeting. "Drew mentioned he came to apologize for something with Nico."

"It was the boys' sophomore year. Drew wanted to do the right thing after bullying and upsetting Nico. I was ready to simply accept his apology and let the little troublemaker go. I figured once a bully always a bully, but I saw something in him as he stood there looking miserable, like he hoped the earth would swallow him whole. So I told him he could make it up by working at The Siren. I never set a time length, and he never left."

"That definitely sounds like him. Stubborn, but committed."

"I watched him grow up. He has passion and focus as most driven men do, but I've always had doubts about the work he chose. Not once since he left

169

here has he truly sounded happy. This was my chance to prove myself right."

"You are a slippery one, Angelo."

"Yes, I am," he said with pride.

"Drew has no idea."

"No, and he's not going to. I didn't exactly lie about the situation here. I did need the break, even wanted one, but it wasn't the emergency I let Drew think it was. I knew he'd come because he wanted to help. He'd never do it for himself, but he'd do it for me and hopefully in the process, he'd see he has other options."

"He does enjoy cooking. I've seen it both here and at home."

"Home?"

She looked down at her coffee. "Can you always get people to say what they would rather hold back?"

"Another gift of age, but don't feel bad. Drew slipped, too, and told me you've been together almost constantly since you met."

"We have and since you know, I'll tell you it's been magical. I love being with him even when he's busy. You'd think after a night of cooking the last place he'd want to be is the kitchen, but depending on what time we wake, he either makes us breakfast or lunch and has a great time doing it."

"So you are enjoying yourself here?"

"Very much."

"Then why are you still planning to leave on Tuesday?"

For the first time in their conversation Lyria was able to keep from blurting out too much truth. Telling Angelo she was a mermaid who needed to return to her people might be a good reason to leave, but it didn't mean she could tell him. Still, she had to give an answer, so she settled for, "My family needs me back. I'm not usually able to get away. This was a special situation."

"More special than you anticipated, I imagine."

"More than I can say, Angelo." As tears started to well in her eyes she excused herself to go back to work, not wanting to reveal anything else to Angelo or dwell on what a mess she was making out of her time here—and what it would cost her in the end. Tears were rare in mermaids, Amina not included. And a very bad sign.

* * *

Since she had asked, Drew allowed Jody to close the restaurant for them and he and Lyria were done early. They spent the rest of the day relaxing, walking along the beach, and swimming. Drew bought her something called a bikini when she told him she had no beachwear. It was the first time she'd ever been in the water with something more than the Band on her. It was odd and uncomfortable at first, but the heated glances Drew sent her way made up for that.

They couldn't decide what to do for dinner. Drew offered to cook, but Lyria pointed out he was doing plenty already with more to come in the days ahead. Unfortunately, trying to choose a restaurant proved to be a challenge. They both wanted something different than the usual Siren fare. Finally, they walked a few blocks away from the boardwalk and brought home little containers of Chinese food. They brought everything out to eat picnic style on the porch, which overlooked the ocean. Lyria thought the packaging was wonderful only to discover the food inside was even better. They ordered noodles, dumplings, and General Gau's chicken, along with rice and cookies with paper in them. It was strange and wonderful. She loved it all. She even tried using the sticks that came with the meal, but no matter how much Drew tried to explain how to use them, she couldn't get the hang of it. She finally gave up and used them to pull back her hair.

After they were done, Drew brought out pillows and blankets and they lay together watching the stars fill the sky. The lights of the town meant there weren't a lot to see, but it was enough and they were far enough away from others for Lyria to feel as though they were alone in the world.

Needing to be closer to him, she removed her dress, then unbuttoned his shirt and took it off. She loved the feel of his chest and his muscles. Using her hands, her hair, and her mouth, she caressed and excited him. She ached to give him the pleasure he offered so freely to her.

Working her way down his body, she covered him in kisses. When she arrived at the waist of his shorts, she unbuttoned and removed them quickly, along with his underwear, anxious to have him naked before her. He was already hard. She exposed his cock and ran her tongue around the tip, enjoying his moan. She understood how exceptionally responsive he was there. The foreskin kept the tip from being out in the open on a regular basis, as her fins did for her. When he was exposed, he was more sensitive than the circumcised men she'd experienced. It was wildly thrilling for her.

Taking him fully into her mouth, she breathed in

his unique scent. He filled her senses. She briefly opened her thoughts up to his emotions and was pleased at the wave of passion which swept over her. It made her hungrier for him, and she took him deeper into her mouth.

"God, Lyria, I can't believe how good that feels."

She didn't answer, simply let her actions show him how much she enjoyed what she was doing. Everything exciting him caused a surge in his cock, which encouraged her to continue. He told her often how he loved her responsiveness. She doubted he realized she loved his as well.

She released his cock from her mouth to lick up and down the shaft with the flat of her tongue, bathing him in its warmth while the cool night air teased him. With her fingers she teased and caressed his balls, and from his moans, she could tell it added to his pleasure. The increased moisture at the tip of his cock told her he was getting closer to his peak.

Once again she took him fully into her mouth, as deeply as she could, relaxing her throat until her lips reached the base. Being filled by him, in any way, was exquisite. She slid her mouth back a bit to grip the bottom of his shaft with her hand and together with her mouth began rhythmically pumping him. His hips lifted, telling her she'd found the right combination. When his hand threaded through her hair, pulling her close, she focused all her attention on his pleasure.

"Lyria, I'm going to come."

She didn't stop what she was doing, pleasuring him as he climaxed in her mouth, taking in every drop of his orgasm. She loved the salty-sweet taste of him, so much like the sea, yet richer and definitely more tantalizing. Moments after he relaxed she continued to flick her tongue around his shaft.

"What are you doing?" he asked.

"I would think it was fairly obvious," she said, taking his cock from her mouth and stroking it with one finger.

"Well, yes, but I'm not used to this continuing beyond an orgasm."

"Does it feel good?"

"Absolutely."

"Then why should I stop? I didn't take you into my mouth with a goal in mind. I'm doing this to please you. Simply because you arrived in one spot you wanted to reach, doesn't mean the journey is over."

She resumed licking him, reveling in his sighs and the knowledge she was doing something for him, giving something to him no female ever had. He was always so ready to satisfy her. It was exciting to offer this pleasure to him. When he became overly responsive and couldn't handle any more, she released him and kissed her way up his body, letting her hair trail over his sensitive skin.

"I knew a woman's long hair was sexy to look at, but I've never had someone brush it over me the way you do. It feels wonderful."

"I'm glad you like it," she said, settling herself next to him, her head comfortably on his chest.

They lay naked on the roof, bathing in the light of the nearly full moon and the aftermath of pleasure, and she sighed with happiness. She refused to think about the days to come.

He suddenly sat up and kissed her. "I have a surprise for you."

"Really?" She wasn't used to good surprises, but his tone sounded excited.

"I bought you something when you were finishing dressing after getting your bikini," Drew said.

"That wasn't necessary."

"I know, but I did it anyway. Stay here and I'll get it."

As if she could move, Lyria thought. Her body felt weightless, not unlike the way it did in the water. If it weren't for the breeze, she might have believed she was swimming somewhere tropical.

He sat down beside her, and she was glad he was still naked. Normally he put on a pair of shorts when he left their bed. She liked him better this way. "I saw it in a window of one of the shops on the boardwalk and couldn't resist. It's funny, normally I don't pay any attention to the places around here since I assume they're all for tourists, but for some reason I was looking closer. Must be because of you."

"Me?"

"Yes, this place is new to you and you look at it with fresh eyes. It's helped me to see it in a way I never have. Guess I've been more jaded than even I thought."

She opened the small-hinged box and her heart rate accelerated at what was inside. Nestled on a bed of black material was a mermaid, gracefully swimming, reaching up and holding a light blue gem in her hand. "It's lovely," she said and meant it, although she was unnerved by the insightful purchase.

"It made me think of you. The times we've gone swimming together, you almost seem more at home in

175

the water than on land. When I remembered the space on your bracelet, I knew I had to get it for you."

Her hand automatically went to the open area beneath the Stone of Clarity. She thought of Amina and the day she gave her the charm. "I can't believe you bought it for me," she said. "I can't remember the last time someone gave me a gift."

"Not even for birthdays?"

She shrugged her shoulders. "It's not our way."

"Well, it's my way, and I hope you like it."

"I do, very much," she said and meant it.

"May I add it to your bracelet?"

"Yes, please." She leaned forward and held her write out to him. He opened the clasp on the charm and hooked it on one of the strands of gold. When the bracelet again settled on her skin, she could feel the cool metal of the new addition and thought the bracelet seemed somehow lighter.

As they kissed she felt a surge of energy go through her arm and body. She looked at the stone and saw it was glowing from within. She was grateful Drew's eyes were shit. She couldn't explain glowing jewelry. She didn't even know why it was doing that.

Before she could determine if it was real or an illusion, Drew put his hand behind her back and pulled her forward into a kiss. Naked, her breasts were soon pressed against his chest and her arms came around his back, deepening the embrace.

Her body responded quickly, as it always did for him, and soon her hand was teasing his cock, wanting him as ready again for sex as she was. He hardened beneath her touch and was soon reaching for a condom with one hand while he fingered her clit with the other.

Her body became wetter for him and he moaned when her wetness touched his fingertips.

"I love how freely you respond," he said.

"I love how you always know exactly what to do about it."

"I love how excited you make me."

"Again we agree."

He smiled, sheathed himself first with the condom and then her body. She tightened around him, bringing him further into her. They moved together as fluidly as the waves breaking nearby and when they came it was so close to together it was hard to know when one started and the other stopped. Or who came first.

After their skin cooled, Drew stood, scooped Lyria up in his arms and carried her to the bedroom. She leaned her head against his shoulder and looked through the window at the moon, hoping the next few days passed safely—and slowly.

The next morning, as Drew went out to get them something for breakfast, the refrigerator was empty, Lyria lay on the bed looking at the bracelet. Its weight was so much more than the gold and gems which made up the chain and charms. Had her uncle been blessed with daughters instead of sons, this burden would not be hers, and she would be free to make her own choices and live her own life. And she never would have met Drew. He was so special. And he'd given her a gift.

Now, after years, an empty space in the string of charms was filled.

Thanks to a human.

Never could Lyria have imagined this. Nor could

177

she have imagined how right the small mermaid looked next to the large Stone of Clarity. Lyria looked again at the beautiful mermaid, letting it rest on her finger. It was as long as the first two joints and the detail was amazing. Whoever created it did so with love and care. In its new position, with the tiny blue gem held in her outstretched hand, it almost appeared as though she were reaching for the Stone, bringing something to it, or taking something from it. Lyria wasn't quite sure which, although it probably didn't matter.

She marveled at Drew's choice, thinking it was as her uncle once told her: you cannot hide your true nature. Drew's nature, even if he didn't know it, was generous and kind. He would not take it well if he discovered her deception. It would be better when she left without telling him.

Still, she would keep this on the Band as a reminder of what they shared and all he offered her. As she stared at the charm, she imagined she saw it move, but knew there was no magic in the world of man to make that happen.

She reminded herself nothing was supposed to matter other than her role and her duties. Nothing could change her destiny to be a part a world that did not include him.

Chapter Eight

Monday, Second day after the full moon

"We're only open for dinner tonight. No club. And one of the advantages of working nights," Drew said, "is doing things during the day other people can't."

She trailed her hand suggestively over his naked chest. "Such as?"

"Going to the movies."

It wasn't what she had expected him to suggest, but she was delighted. "I haven't seen one in years," she said. The year after her Band ceremony, she'd sneaked away and seen and action movie called *Wanted.* She loved every minute of it, but she'd been in such trouble on her return for being out of communication's reach that she had never dared go again. There was something in particular she remembered from the experience. "I want my own popcorn."

"You love the salty stuff, don't you?"

"Everyone's got a weakness," she said.

"Mine seems to be you." He kissed her and she allowed herself to melt into the embrace, thinking he was much better than any salty treat.

They saw a new movie called *Wonder Woman,* which was very good. She liked the heroine, from one world, defending another. She enjoyed being snuggled against Drew almost as much, if not more, than the movie. They were walking back to The Siren, when she froze.

Lyria, I need to talk to you came an urgent voice in her head.

She replied immediately, thinking, *Amina, what's wrong?* There was no way Amina would risk being overheard using long-distance telepathic ability unless there was a serious problem. It was too intrusive to accidently hear or see the thoughts of the other. During their younger years it caused problems and a few uncomfortable situations.

I'm not sure but if I see you in person I'll be able to figure it out.

She sent her cousin an image of the rocks. *I'll be there tonight. We can talk then.*

Take care of yourself, Lyria. Something isn't right.

I will, my sweet.

"Are you okay?" Drew asked, bringing her back to the moment.

"Yes, fine," she said. "Why do you ask?"

"You looked about 100 miles away."

It was closer to 200 or 300, she thought, but she didn't say anything. "Just wondering about what we need to do when we get back."

"It's Monday, so hopefully things will be pretty light. Not a big night for going out. We do a lot of ordering, scheduling and reorganizing that can't be done during the madness of the weekend."

"Wondering how he would react, she said, "That's good because I'm meeting a friend later tonight."

"You didn't mention this earlier, did you?"

"No, it's someone who got in touch and is passing through."

"Invite him to The Siren. Dinner's on me."

"It's a her," she said. His use of the male pronoun was interesting, but she didn't know if it was his way of trying to discover if she was meeting with another man. "She's not staying long, so I doubt we'll have a chance to drop by."

"No problem."

It frustrated her when she couldn't read his tone and couldn't tell if he meant what he said. This was happening with increasing frequency. When they had first met, she could sense everything from him, but the longer they were together, the more she was at a loss to figure out what he was thinking or feeling. Perhaps spending time on land was dimming some of her sensory abilities. She hoped when she returned to the sea, things would return to normal.

Unfortunately, she had a suspicion that even when she went home, normal was not going to be the same as it was when she left.

When they got back to The Siren, Lyria went upstairs to relax while Drew went to check on messages and deliveries.

She lay on the bed—their bed—thinking of all they shared and tracing the Stone in its setting. She allowed her fingers to warm it, as its vibrations of energy ran through her. Even after ten years, she didn't know exactly how to activate all of its powers, but as long as it was close to her, against her skin, she could reassure herself no harm would come to the world she loved.

She remembered one of her previous encounters with the Sea Dragon, not long before his claim of betrothal. She was miles away from him when he linked with her, but his telepathy was so powerful she could not block the words or images he sent to her.

"I will destroy you, Lyria, but only after I kill everyone you care about and make certain you are a witness. Then you will know you have lost and any hope you have of escape will be as dead as your loved ones." He showed her visions of her cousin being ripped apart, patients tied down and ravaged by carnivorous fish, even a former lover being burned in boiling water. The images were horrifying, the message clear. But it wasn't the message he wanted her to get.

He wanted her to be so afraid she'd turn over the gem and her freedom to save them. But any creature who could consider doing these vile things could not be trusted, and certainly not allowed to be connected to the Stone of Clarity. If anything, it made her more determined than ever to keep it from him. Amina, too, was careful, staying clear of her usual haunts or not traveling there alone. The easiest way to hurt one was through the other, so they did what was necessary to remain safe and checked in with each other regularly.

Which brought her back to her cousin's earlier communication. Something must be seriously wrong if she wanted not only to talk to Lyria but to see her face to face. A knot formed in Lyria's stomach as she tried to think of what the problem might be. She stopped herself and took a deep breath. Imagining the worst was not only a waste of energy, but rarely led to a productive outcome. It would feel like forever, but she would wait until this evening, hear what Amina had to say, and move forward from there.

No amount of deep breathing helped. By the time she went to a secluded spot, she was a bundle of nerves.

"Don't shift," Amina said, breaking through the waves as Lyria was preparing to dive in.

"Hello to you too, Amina."

"Sorry, pleasantries are not on my mind."

"Clearly. Why shouldn't I change?"

"Because it could be dangerous. Have you been doing it often?"

"Amina, you're not making any sense."

"I will in a second, but for now, please tell me, when was the last time you finned?"

Lyria had to think. Drew was busy and she snuck out to the water on her break. "Yesterday. I had a long day and I needed the freedom of the waves, of distance."

Amina shook her head. "Then that can't be it. I guess it's fine for you to join me."

"Thanks for the permission, but would you mind letting me know why the questions?"

"You're being tracked."

"Yes, I know. Fiero is looking for me. This is not news."

"But there have been times recently when you've been"—she paused, searching for the words—"easier to sense."

"How do you know?"

"Because I've been able to feel you during those

183

times. Please, let's come away from here and I'll tell you everything."

Lyria placed her dress in her bag and slid naked into the water, fully finned by the time she surfaced. *Let's go,* she said and they started swimming.

Twenty minutes later they were miles away and came ashore on a small outcropping of land. "Start from the beginning, Amina."

"Are you certain you're okay?"

"Don't I look it? I'm fine. It's been a very uneventful few days. Why? What have you learned?"

"Two days ago, Uncle's guards intercepted a tracker naiad on his way to report to Fiero with news he had sensed you in the Mid-Atlantic region. They brought the naiad to court where Aunt Betta used a truth potion to force him to tell all he knew." Lyria knew that was serious. Truth potions were rarely used as compulsion was not considered an appropriate action. "Your injury from your last encounter resulted in a significant loss of blood." Lyria ran her fingers over the scar on her hip. "It seems Fiero collected the water with your blood and has given it to his minions so they can track you."

Lyria shuddered involuntarily. "There's something else," she said. "I can see it in your eyes."

Amina nodded, "When he was pushed to the truth, the naiad spoke of the sea dragon sensing you, something I have recently as well. Once there was a feeling of panic and fear. The next time there's a warm rush, a glow of something lovely and free and distinctly you. I thought it was you reaching out to me, letting me know you were fine. When I heard him mention this, I had to track you."

"You could have been followed."

"Don't worry about me. I have a few things to cover my trail and distract anyone or anything that might be watching me. Fiero tried to get me too."

"Goddess help us. When was this?"

"Yesterday and as you can see I'm fine. Truly. And even though it was a horrible situation, it was good to learn that Fiero has spies within our staff. There's been a lot of interviewing going on to find the traitors. And like you, I've been keeping hidden as well, but Aunt Betta reached out and asked me to come I when the naiad was caught."

"I'm not sure that makes me feeling batter."

"Everyone wants to keep us safe, Lyria. It's why I had to take the risk and find you. I knew it was likely that whatever caused the feeling was happening involuntarily. I had to come and let you know, to see if it was something that could be stopped. I assumed it was when you came off land and took your mermaid form, but now it doesn't seem to be the case."

Lyria took a deep breath and tried to think logically. "So we know Fiero is using my blood as well as naiads to track me."

"And something you are doing or thinking is sending out a stronger signal than usual which may allow him to find you before we can stop it."

"Wonderful. Any more good news?"

"Wilmar one of the traitors who tried to abduct me. He got away."

"Amina, I'm sorry I ever brought him into my life. Our lives. He's been one problem after another. And now he's a real danger to us."

"Hopefully not for much longer. With any luck

when we find Fiero and end that threat, Wilmar will be found as well."

Lyria sent up a prayer of hope. "If it's not shifting that intensifies my signal, what does?"

"I'm afraid I have no answer, Lyria." Amina thought for a moment. "What were you doing late last night? That was the last time I felt it."

Lyria thought back to the previous day and an image of being naked under the moon and wrapped around Drew came to her mind. She remembered her screams as she climaxed from his attentions. It was fortunate, she thought, that she, unlike Amina didn't blush. "I was with a man," she answered vaguely.

"Clearly he pleased you."

"Yes."

"And is he special to you?"

"Of course not," Lyria said almost too quickly and her sister raised an eyebrow, a motion Lyria hated, in part because she could not do it too. "He's a good man, even for a human."

"You're falling for him."

"I'm not, Amina, you know me better. I'm enjoying my time with him but tomorrow as the moon passes its third waning day, I will be leaving." She hated hearing the words.

"I don't doubt that is what you believe, or at least still hope, but I think there is something about this man. He is affecting you, perhaps even changing you."

"It's not possible," Lyria said.

"Was last night the only night you made love?"

"No, it's been fairly regular these last few days."

"Then that's not it."

"I don't know what it could be then," said Lyria.

186

Then she remembered something else. The charm. The golden mermaid he added to the bracelet and the electric warmth she felt after. She told Amina and showed her the charm.

"You received a gift. From a human. And he chose a mermaid."

"That's pretty much how my thought process went, too."

"Okay, I'm going let this sink in later. Another times the stone responded to something?"

"I was attacked on the Boardwalk."

"What?" Amina looked horrified.

"By humans, not naiads. They tried to steal the bracelet and it… protected me."

"Protected you how?"

She explained to Amina about the surge of power throwing the men away and knocking them unconscious.

"So when the stone is activated for any reason, you can be sensed more easily."

"At least be those who are connect to me by blood—or in contact with my blood."

"Now we know. I don't know if that's helpful, but I'm relieved it's not something as simple as finning. Or sex."

"Don't push it."

Amina reached over and pulled Lyria into her arms and kissed the top of her head. "I'm sorry. I should not make fun. I know how difficult your situation is."

Lyria said nothing, and simply allowed Amina to comfort her. It was not a position she often allowed herself to be in, or that was often offered to her. She was surprised by how welcoming it was. But she still needed to be shielded better, at least for a little while longer.

"Maybe there's another way to protect you," Amina said.

"Peering into my thoughts? We said we wouldn't do that to one another, remember?"

"I have no need of peering in this moment. Your thoughts are as clear to me as the sea. In fact, I was, for once, able to anticipate that you might need some assistance."

"Is that so?" Lyria said. "What a nice change." Growing up, Lyria often pointed out to Amina how often she needed Lyria's help rather than the other way around.

"It happens," Amina said. She produced a small clear bottle in a teardrop shape. Within the tear swirled a dark gray liquid. Something about it made Lyria uncomfortable. "I have this from Nerine."

Lyria was truly shocked. The daughter of a mermaid and a lamia, Nerine's power was legendary despite her relatively young age. Her temper was equally fearful. She kept to herself and it was rumored most who sought her help never returned. "You visited Nerine? Does Uncle know?"

The pause told Lyria plenty. "I believe so since Aunt Betta recommended it. Nerine, it seems brews very powerful magic and she was the most logical person to see. I found her earlier today, received this, and then I headed here. After we're done, it's my turn to find a place to be safe."

"You could have been killed."

"It was worth the risk, although I never sensed any danger."

Lyria's throat closed over any further protest. If the situation were reversed, she'd do the same.

"Interestingly, I didn't find her as frightening as her reputation," Amina said. "In fact, I think she may have created the stories to allow her privacy, scare off the weak."

"What does the potion do?"

"It covers you, acts as a shield of sorts. Nerine said you must drink it quickly and in one swallow and it should hinder Fiero or his minions from finding you. I had her create a bottle for both of us, which I've already taken. Not knowing what was causing your sensory visibility, and having already been attacked once, I thought better safe than sorry. It's why I am almost certain I haven't been tracked. It does have a side effect—your healing gifts will be temporarily blocked as well."

"That's quite a side effect." Lyria looked at the bottle. "Wait, does that mean…"

"Yes, for the moment your emotions are completely unreadable to me."

"Are you sure that's wise?"

"It's the lesser to two evils," Amina said.

"In this situation, I sadly have to agree."

"I still can't believe you received a gift from your human friend and that it's now part of the bracelet. He must be very special."

"He is a special person, but not particularly to me."

"My gift is knowing others feelings, Lyria, and I may not be able to sense your emotions because of the potions but I can see them in your eyes. You may want to lie to yourself, but you can't lie to me. Not even

Nerine could create a potion which could change that. Speaking of which, you have to drink it while the bottle still feels warm. If it's gone cold, the magic is gone."

"Thank you."

They hugged and wished each other well. Amina left for parts unknown. Lyria returned to The Siren.

Lyria wondered if she visited Nerine after leaving New Jersey, the mermaid could brew something which would make her feelings for Drew disappear.

* * *

The smells of boardwalk food while Lyria was walking along the beach over her private island made it clear to Lyria she was dreaming. The two didn't go together. She tried to push away the sadness that overwhelmed her as she thought about trying to connect both places. As soon as the final day passed she would no longer be able to enjoy the Jersey Shore or, more importantly, spend time with Drew, and the knowledge made her ache. Even in this fantasy realm.

She walked into the shallow water, sat so the waves lapped her, and allowed her body to fin. Looking at the scales as they caught the sun, she wondered what Drew would say if he saw her this way.

History told her how humans reacted to the true form of merfolk. It was one of the few places where the stories and the reality matched, but in this dream Lyria could admit to herself she wanted Drew to be different, wanted their story to be different. She longed to tell him of her loneliness, her isolation, and how she ached to connect. The burden of the Band wouldn't be as weighty if there were someone special in her life who understood, someone she could share her life with.

She didn't realize she'd spoken out loud until someone said, "Who is Drew?"

Lyria shifted to legs and stood, looking around for the man—the dragon—that went with the voice. "Where are you? Show yourself"

"Wishing for your own fairy tale happy ending?"

She ran back to her home only to find she was now in The Siren and he was sitting at Angelo's table. "Why have I conjured you in this place? You don't belong here."

"You are quite right about the latter," said Fiero. "But let me dissuade you from the former. You didn't conjure me." He reached out for her so fast she had no time to react. His hand grasped her around the wrist and twisted painfully. She screamed and dropped to her knees.

"Let me go." How could something happening in a dream hurt so much.

"Nerine is not the only ocean being with magical gifts. There are those who have access to dark and powerful magic—including the ability to connect with someone while they sleep."

She let his words sink in. "You found the Angler Witch." The Angler Witch was more elusive than Nerine, an Oceanide of dark magic. Dreams were her reputed realm.

"I did. You didn't think I'd come after the Stone of Clarity without a strong plan and even stronger magic on my side?"

"Truthfully, I didn't think you'd be foolish

enough to come after the Stone at all. It will never be yours, and neither will I."

"Oh, no? You don't think I can find you or this Drew you care so much about?"

"You leave him out of this. He has nothing to do with you or what you are after."

"But of course he does. He's a link to you, as well as a possible weakness, and if you don't think I'm going to exploit everything in my power, you have underestimated me."

"I have done no such thing, Fiero. I am simply suggesting you don't bother him, because should you harm him in any way it will be your end."

She didn't know where the words were coming from—or if she could back them up—but she was compelled to say them. They felt true, although she couldn't explain why.

"Such bravado. I will find you, healer. You are releasing some sort of signal. Between that and the fact I have your blood, I will find you. And if not, there is always your cousin to be used as bait. Amina is such a pretty little thing. You wouldn't want anything to happen to her, would you?"

Lyria screamed and lunged at him but before she could reach him, she woke up with a gasp. In her mind she heard Fiero's frustration. Clearly he was annoyed she'd left the dream so soon. She smiled, glad to have thwarted at least part of his plan. She didn't know if there was anything she could do to keep him out for the next days, but she would do what she could.

"Are you okay?" She jumped at Drew's voice and he put his arm around her. "I'll take that as a no. Bad dream?"

She nodded. "Unexpected." She thought about the potion in her bag. Should she take it now?

"Sorry to hear. Should I turn the light on? Want to talk about it?"

"No, it's not necessary. The moon is bright enough, and I'm awake now. Whatever it was that scared me is gone."

"And I'm here."

"Which is particularly nice." She curled against him enjoying the feel of him next to her.

"Your skin is always so cool."

There was no way to tell him it was a result of living most of her life in the ocean. "Which works well because you're always so warm."

"As long as you're not chilly."

"Not in the least."

"I could warm you up a little," he said.

"You could warm me up a lot." She rolled him on top of her and kissed him. "You're a great blanket."

He laughed. "I don't think I've ever been called that before, but thanks."

"You're very welcome." She rolled her hips under him and his erection pressed against her thigh. She wanted to be close to him, to forget about Fiero and his threats. He wouldn't have invaded her dream if he didn't need information, and she was nearly certain he gleaned nothing from their short time together. Amina was smart and well protected. The potion was forgotten.

For now, she was safe in Drew's bed.

In his arms.

Which, as much as it surprised her, was exactly where she wanted to be.

Chapter Nine

Tuesday, Third day after the full moon

From the moment she woke, Lyria sensed the ticking of the clock. Her time here was nearly over, and even if she didn't know what Fiero had planned, she knew without a doubt he would be doing whatever he could to find her.

They didn't talk about this being her final day, but Lyria knew from Drew's plans he was thinking about her leaving as much as she was. After a late breakfast they did all things on the boardwalk she loved best, starting at the roller coaster, moving to skeeball and ending with frozen custard, which remained her favorite treat. Stanley had come back, interested in doing lunch shifts only, so they weren't due at The Siren until four. They swam, walked along the edge of the waves, kissed, and laughed. When they finally came in, they made love before taking a quick shower together and arriving at the restaurant shortly before the shift change.

By the time she pulled her hair back, put her uniform on and heard about the day's specials, the first dinner guests were arriving. Her last guests. She hoped when she returned home, she would take back some of what she learned about being with people and the simple joy of giving them what they wanted. It would make her time here even more special.

Fifteen minutes into her shift, a rare solo diner was seated at one of her tables. She put a smile on her face as she walked over. "Welcome to The Siren, sir. Can I get you a drink while you're looking at the menu?"

"A beer, something American and on tap."

"Absolutely. Would you like to hear our specials?"

"Sure."

She recited them, telling him which was her favorite, then left to get him his drink. When she came back he already knew what he wanted and gave her an order the fried calamari appetizer and the chicken with citrus salsa.

"Is Drew in the back?"

"Yes."

"I heard through the grapevine he's doing the cooking."

"Yes, sir. Do you know him?"

"I'm Sam, his father."

Lyria almost dropped her order pad. So this was the man who caused Drew such confusion and anger. Looking at the older man, she didn't see much of resemblance except for the same deep gray eyes.

"I'm guessing from your look of surprise you know Drew."

"I do."

"And you know even though he's been back for four months, I haven't seen him."

"I didn't know the specifics, sir, but yes, I knew you didn't speak much."

He gave a bitter laugh and took a swallow of his beer. "That's an understatement."

"Do you want me to tell him you're here?"

"No, not just yet. But thanks."

Lyria nodded. "I'll put your order in. The calamari should be up quickly."

She went into the kitchen, placed the order where Drew and the others could see it, then left as quickly as she could to help at other tables so as not to have to talk to Drew. She didn't trust herself to keep the surprise off her face and the concern out of her voice.

She walked around the restaurant, trying to keep busy, but it was too early in the evening for there to be many customers.

"Another beer?" she asked when she brought Sam his calamari.

"No, one is my limit these days, along with a lot fewer fried foods," he said, motioning to the appetizer. He took a bite and sighed. "Ah, but they are worth every bite."

His smile was so much like Drew's she couldn't help but return it. "I'm glad you like it, sir."

"Sam."

"Sam, then."

"Have you known him long?" She knew who he met.

"Only a few days." Sam didn't say anything. "He's a great guy."

"I know." He popped another calamari in his mouth and said, "Of course, he doesn't believe I see it, but I do."

"I hope you'll tell him."

"Bold one, aren't you?"

"Sometimes we have to tell people the truth, no matter how hard it is." She tried not to listen to her own words, but they were too close to her heart to ignore.

He stared into the foam of his empty glass. "Maybe I should order a second beer after all."

"I bet you'll be fine without it."

He remained silent. Lyria put a hand on his as a gesture of comfort, but the brief contact ended up giving her information she didn't expect. As she assisted other guests, she couldn't stop thinking about Sam and Drew. She hoped something positive would come out of his visit today, because the older man was dying. Lyria didn't know if Sam knew his own diagnosis, but the cancer was advanced.

"I think you're going to like this," she said when she brought him his chicken.

He looked at the beautifully plated meal in confusion. "I've never ordered anything so—colorful."

She smiled. "It's the fruit salsa. Trust me, it's divine."

"I'm usually a steak and potatoes kind of guy. It's a stereotype, I know, but what the hell."

She's not sure what that meant to she simply smiled and said, "I hope you enjoy it."

The place was getting busier so by the time she came back to Sam to refill his water, he was nearly done. "You were right. It was excellent."

"Would you like to compliment the chef?"

He didn't respond immediately, but Lyria was willing to wait. "Yes. I would."

"I'll get him for you."

She was nervous when she went into the kitchen.

She found Drew working on two different dishes. "Can you take a break for a little bit?"

He gave her a sexy smile, "For you, anything."

"Wonderful, although this is not for me. The guest at table four wants to compliment you on your cooking."

"Well, you're more fun, but I'll take the positive feedback for now." He washed his hands, came around to where she stood, and grabbed her around the waist as he kissed her neck. "And I'll take you later."

"No arguments from me." She followed him out, then stopped as he went the rest of the way himself. She watched his pace change when he saw Sam. For a moment she thought he might turn around and come back without saying anything, but after a moment he continued to the table.

* * *

If he didn't see him with his own eyes, he'd never believe it. His father was sitting there, eating his cooking. He couldn't remember Sam ever setting foot in The Siren. "Hi, Dad."

"Hello, Drew. I'm sure you're busy but would you sit for a minute?"

Drew was surprised by the request and how unsure his dad sounded. Nothing like what he expected. He was used to short clipped sentences. Orders. Annoyance. "I hear you enjoyed your meal."

"I think this was the first time I didn't order prime rib at a restaurant. The chicken special came highly recommended." He pointed a chin in Lyria's direction.

198

"And?"

"I liked it. Never would have thought fruit and chicken would go together, but it was really good."

He hardly knew how to respond to the compliment, but he managed a quiet, "Thanks."

"You've been back a while."

"I figured you'd hear."

"Guess things in the city didn't work out like you planned."

Drew gave a smirk and a short bitter laugh. Didn't take long for his dad to start in. Well, he was not going to make a scene, no matter how his dad might try to provoke him. "Since I wasn't planning to fail, clearly not."

"So you came back."

"Mr. V. called and needed help."

"You always were close to him."

He wasn't going to take the bait. Well, maybe a little. "He listened to me."

"I listened to you."

"No you didn't, Dad. You argued with me and told me my ideas were ridiculous and I should forget them."

Sam fiddled with his fork, pushing around the small remaining pieces of his meal. "Guess that wasn't the right thing to say."

"Oh, I don't know. I'm back here and the things I tried were a failure. Congratulations, you were right. That should make you happy?"

"Happy? Of course not. Why would I want you to fail, Drew? Your being miserable would never make me happy. No parent wishes that. You are so different from your brother. I was afraid for you because I couldn't prepare you. I couldn't make you strong. Do you really think I wanted you to go through this?"

It was Drew's turn for not having an answer. "I don't know. I don't think you wished for me to fuck up, only that you expected it."

"I always expected you would be amazing, and completely beyond me and your brother. You were always talking about things I didn't understand."

"Or didn't want to understand."

Sam nodded in acknowledgement. "That could be true. I didn't like my son being so much smarter. Figured you'd end up looking down on me. Guess that happened anyway." He paused before continuing. "We're not really good at this, are we?"

"At what?"

"Talking to each other."

"Not at a normal volume, no," agreed Drew.

"I'm sorry."

Drew thought this conversation couldn't get stranger, but he was wrong.

His dad continued, "You started having ideas and plans that I knew nothing about, and I was at a complete loss about how to support you," his father said. "Your mother was the one with the big dreams. She would have known what to do, what to say."

Drew was surprised Sam brought up his mother. He rarely spoke of her after she died when Drew was ten. Talking to his father was turning out to be tougher than not talking. "I didn't think you wanted to support me since I didn't want what you wanted."

"Yeah, I can see how it sounded like that. I didn't like how you saw me as some dumb failure. All I knew was life on the Jersey Shore and construction. It wasn't the easiest life, but it worked for me, took care of you boys, and put a roof over our heads."

Drew heard Mr. V.'s words echoed in his fathers. He never expected the two men to have the same opinion on anything.

"The thought of you out in the unknown, where I couldn't do anything for you, scared the shit out of me," Sam said.

His father's reactions and words stemmed from fear? It was something Drew had never considered. "That was your way of protecting me?"

"It's all I knew. Hey, those were the days before Dr. Phil. I thought I had to be tough on you and Michael or you'd never make it in the real world. Dreams were great, but not if you got your teeth kicked in."

"You watched Dr. Phil?"

He shrugged and gave a slight laugh. "Sometimes, you know, when we're between jobs, and there was nothing else on."

Drew smiled at the image. It didn't fit with the man he remembered. Then again, neither did any of this. "I guess I didn't understand you any more than you understood me."

"No, I suppose not."

"I'm sorry I acted like I thought you were dumb. That was unfair of me," Drew said, taking a sip from a water glass he didn't notice appear in front of him. "So, now what do we do?"

"Not a clue."

"Me either, so I guess we agree on something. That has to be good."

"I really did want to tell you the food was great."

"Thanks. Which reminds me, why did you order the chicken?"

"Doctor says I've got to watch what I eat. Seems all the food I like has been clogging up my arteries and stuff."

"I hear it happens."

"Would you mind if I came in every now and then? To see you and have you do the cooking? I've never been very good at it."

"I'd like that," Drew said and he was surprised to realize he meant it.

"How long are you staying?"

"I don't know."

And that truth surprised him most of all.

* * *

Lyria was waiting for Drew when he came into the kitchen. Instead of saying anything, she reached out with her senses and received a sense of calm and touch of happiness. She took her first deep breath since meeting Sam. "I'm glad you two spoke."

"So am I," he said. "To say it was unexpected would be a huge understatement. We may have a chance at some kind of relationship."

"That's wonderful."

"You know, I think so too." He kissed her and held her close, her head under his chin. "Some really amazing things have happened since you arrived. I don't suppose you'd consider staying and seeing what happens next, would you?"

She didn't respond. She couldn't see how to make it work.

"Sorry, I guess I shouldn't have asked. I'm on a bit of a high right now."

She looked up at him and felt joy mixed with sadness. "Kiss me."

"Gladly."

Lyria poured all her emotion into the kiss, hoping she could show him how much she cared, how she loved being with him no matter what her actions might be. She ran her hands through his hair as she tasted him. She wanted to remember everything about him.

"Get a room, you two," said Jody.

"Got one upstairs," Drew said as they pulled apart.

"Then take a break up there or get back here and help. Stop making the single ladies jealous."

"That's my cue," Drew said to Lyria.

"Yes, it is."

"I'd like to talk about this later."

She nodded, knowing there was a good chance she wouldn't be here when he finally had time after his shift. It was the coward's way out, but she was tempted to take it.

Two hours later, while she was on a break, a deep and watery voice called out to her and brought her to the nearest window.

Come out, Mermaid. I know you are close and I know you can hear me.

Chapter Ten

The sun was setting and the beach was nearly empty of the day's visitors. Lyria couldn't see who called her but by extending her senses, she had an idea of where he was.

She'd allowed herself to be lulled into believing she was going to make it through the next hours without being found, but it was not to be. It was always likely Fiero would find her before the third waning day. All she experienced with Drew was worth what she had to face. He would be hurt to find her gone, but at least she would have broken no promises.

Show yourself to me or I will harm the humans among whom you conceal yourself.

She turned back to the window and, while she couldn't see the naiad who called her, she saw a distant wave swell unexpectedly. Lyria was surprised and unnerved by the action. There was a time when those of the sea would not have dared harm those of the land for fear of the consequences. Clearly fear of the Sea Dragon was greater, a thought which did not sit easy with her. If Fiero became whom sea dwellers feared most, then he would also be who they followed. The consequences of not keeping the Stone of Clarity safe continued to grow.

As she left the room, instead of taking one of her

dresses, she threw one of Drew's T-shirts over her head. It felt strangely heavy and awkward on her body as she walked to meet someone from her own world, and brought to mind how ill-fitting this world was for merfolk.

She walked to the edge of the water and let the waves bathe her feet. It would be easy to fin and join the naiad deeper in the ocean, but she wanted to make her opponent come closer to her first. It was important she show bravery, even daring.

"I am here. Where are you, errand boy?"

The naiad rose from the water, remaining covered by the waves from the calves down. Should anyone look, it would be more than a little alarming, but Lyria could not be worried about who might see.

"I am no errand boy," he said. She was pleased he was angered. Angered creatures made mistakes. "I am a member of Fiero's court, and I will be well rewarded when he has the Stone of Clarity and eventually competes Melusine's Band."

"You are a fool who has chosen the wrong side."

"You have that backwards, Mermaid. You are the foolish one to think you can hide from Fiero's power."

"I am not hiding."

"What do you call cowering on land?"

"Keeping something away from the devil is neither hiding nor cowering. It is strategy. Do you honestly believe anything good will happen to those who dwell in the sea if your so-called leader acquires what he wants?"

The naiad paused before answering, and Lyria hoped she'd made a small dent in his bravado. Anything she could use to her advantage, she would. "I have all the proof I need," he said.

"I am certain you do. You don't strike me as someone who needs much of anything, which is good because that is likely to be what you will receive."

Water rose up the body of the naiad, alerting her to his drawing of power. She anticipated and shielded the blast he sent her way, allowing the heavily salted water to fall at her feet. It wasn't a dangerous move, but often distracting, something she would not allow to happen.

"Apparently you are not allowed to kill me, so what it is it you want?"

"You are to come with me or your cousin will die."

"We will all die someday," she said, although a cold feeling of dread crept through her blood.

"She is Fiero's captive, and if you don't come with me and willingly turn over what he wants, she will die a long, slow, horrible, painful death."

"And I am expected to comply simply based on your word?"

"It would make my job easier, but no, I have evidence."

Lyria hoped no change in her emotions could be seen on her face. The same was not true of her thoughts. In his hand was the chain on which the gifted charm from her bracelet dangled. Nothing could compel Amina to take off the necklace, which meant the naiad's words were true. Fiero had Amina. And Lyria had an impossible choice to make.

No, she thought, there was no choice at all. She would rather face a fight with a Sea Dragon than have even a moment of harm come to Amina.

"Very well," she said. "However, how am I to know that even if I go with you, she will not be hurt?"

"I'm afraid you want assurances I cannot give you, Mermaid. Only the Sea Dragon himself can offer you what you want, so once again you must come with me. If we are not there in time for him to take the Stone from you, she will come to a very bad end."

It was an unfortunate point. There was no telling how long they needed to travel and Fiero needed the stone before the moon was at its highest this evening. Lyria tried to think of a strategy that would involve saving Amina without going with the naiad when another challenge arrived.

"Lyria, what are you doing out here?" Drew said. "It's freezing. Gotta love the beginning of summer. Warm one minute, cold again the next. Did I hear you talking to someone?"

"Drew, go back inside. Take care of The Siren." Could he hear the pleading in her voice?

"Come with me," he said and put his arm around her to draw her back to the apartment. Once they touched, the magic shielding the naiad from view would no longer work on Drew. He would be connected to her, able to see what she saw. For the moment, however, he was still looking at her, clearly wanting her to follow.

How she wished she could go. She wanted to let him warm her and take her away from all the responsibilities and loneliness she'd felt for so long, but the setting sun caught a slice of agate in the charm still held out by the naiad, and once again she was painfully aware of how so few choices she truly had. She turned her back on her calling before and Amina almost died.

Never again.

The naiad moved forward, rapidly closing the distance between them. Lyria could see the light of madness in his eyes and automatically moved to put herself in front of Drew. "Tell the human to leave or see him destroyed," he said.

"Who is that?" Drew asked and turned to the ocean before Lyria could stop or distract him. "Okay, let me rephrase. *What* is that?"

"I am the man come to take this mermaid back to where she belongs and to whom she belongs."

"Mermaid? Jesus, what are you on, man?"

The naiad gave an evil laugh. "You have not trusted the human with who you are. Perhaps you are not as foolish as Wilmar thinks."

"Wilmar," she repeated. Hearing the name of the merman who once pursued her was more of a surprise than learning of Amina's capture. "What does he have to do with this?"

The naiad sent a burst of water into the air. Clearly she wasn't supposed to know of Wilmar's involvement. Since it was too late to take back the information, however, the naiad answered the question. "How do you think we knew so much about you? We've been getting information from several sources, but the merman has been particularly helpful. How important your cousin is to you. How your blood helps us to track you. He has been an invaluable resource to the Sea Dragon, and I expect he will be well rewarded once you have returned to your place."

Before Lyria could answer, Drew took her hand. "What is going on? Who is Wilmar and why did that thing out there call you a mermaid?"

"I wish I could explain it all to you, Drew, but I

can't. There's no time. I have to go. They have my cousin. I have what they want, so you see"—her voice broke as she continued—"I have no choice."

"I don't see anything of the sort. I'm pretty certain there's something significant you've been keeping from me, but more importantly, you're leaving. Not only were you are not planning to come back, but you were going to just disappear without saying anything or giving me a chance to ask you to stay. Am I wrong?"

She shook her head, not trusting herself to say anything. The expression on his face made her ache. "I told you my time here was limited."

"I think there's more to the situation than that?"

"Come now, Mermaid," the naiad interrupted. "If I leave without you, you will never find and save your precious Amina."

"You will give me a moment or so help me, I will destroy you the first chance I get." She turned to Drew and placed a hand on his cheek. "I am so sorry for all of this. There is so much I wish I could tell you and show you. I wish I could have more time with you, but that is the story of my life, I'm afraid. I go where I'm told and where I'm needed. Please, don't hate me for having to leave. Don't give up on your dreams or The Siren."

"I am out of patience and time," the naiad yelled. The final rays of the sun caught the light of the rising water. Lyria and Drew turned at the same time to see the naiad pull power from the ocean. Strings of magical current curled around his waist and began to weave a net. He pulled back his hand and forced it forward with a shove.

It was meant to capture her, not harm her, but in the last moment, Drew broke away from her side and moved forward to protect her. Lyria screamed his name as she saw the string of magic change as it hit Drew in the leg. He yelled and collapsed against her, bringing them both crashing to the sand. In the anger which bubbled from within her, Lyria threw a spell toward the naiad and was gratified to see him explode in a shower of droplets. From the sea, returned to the sea.

But what about Amina? Had her emotional response destroyed any possibility of her finding her cousin? An image of the angry Sea Dragon came to her and she calmed. If she put herself out in the open, Fiero would find her. Once he did, she would be able to help Amina.

There was a greater problem to deal with first.

She looked down at her hand which was on Drew's leg and cursed at the sight of the blood seeping through her fingers. One day more and he would have been safe, and she would have been hundreds of miles away. Instead he was badly injured because of her and there was no time to get to a human care facility. Worse, she didn't know if one would be any good, since the gash was caused by magic.

She should leave him here. It had been done to the women in her family time and time again. She could call for help and disappear, and he'd never be able to find or reach her.

The thought made her heart hurt and, unexpectedly, the bracelet began to burn her wrist. Without thinking about it further, she worked to heal him. Projecting her magic out, she covered his injury with a layer of scales. Hoping it was enough to hold him, she dragged them into the ocean and encircled him with her body. She kissed him as she finned and dove deeply into the water and swam as fast as she could.

* * *

Drew regained consciousness but not understanding. He remembered being on the beach with Lyria, who'd been talking to some creature who looked half drowned. No, not talking—arguing. Then the thing attacked her with something that looked to Drew like lightning. He remembered the excruciating pain, then nothing. He must have passed out.

He tried to move, but couldn't. Something was wrapped around him, holding him still. He tried to open his eyes and talk, but couldn't. With a growing sense of panic, he started to lash out in any way possible.

Hold still, Drew. We're almost there and then you can move.

Lyria's voice calmed him until he realized he was hearing it in his head, not with his ears. In fact, all he could hear was a rushing sound reminding him of a strong wind. Or waves.

You are going to be fine. Try to relax. I know it's not easy, but I promise to tell you everything I can as soon as we're somewhere safe.

He was dreaming. Whatever hit him knocked him out and now he was having some sort of post-injury hallucination. Or maybe he was in a hospital and deeply medicated. Still, if she could talk to him this way, then he must be able to do the same. *Where are we going?*

To my place.

That sounded nice. *And where would that be?*
It's a small island off the coast of Florida.

He was right. He remembered when they met, he'd asked where she was from. She did live near Florida. This was a very nice dream. *Is it much further?*

She didn't answer immediately, although he saw underwater images rushing past in his mind. *Only about 20 minutes or so. Rest for a while longer and I'll wake you when we get there.*

Rest sounded good, so he slipped back into what he assumed was sleep. When he woke this time, he sensed a cool breeze on his face. He opened his eyes and saw he was in the bed of a small room with only a few pieces of furniture and little decoration beyond sheer blue curtains the color of the sky, billowing in. Looking down, he saw he was naked and after moving his leg, he discovered he was injured as well. Before he could uncover himself to see his wound, Lyria walked in.

"You're awake. I brought you some water and fruit. Are you hungry?"

"Actually, I am. What time is it?"

"A little after nine." She handed him the glass of water and he drank it quickly. She refilled, it then sat on the bed next to him. "How are you feeling?"

"Not bad, considering the dream I had and the fact I've woken up in a strange place with a rather large bandage on my leg, which is making me wonder if it was a dream at all."

She took his hand in hers. It was cool, as always. "It wasn't a dream, Drew. Everything you saw, felt, and heard was real. And true."

"Then you really are…" He couldn't bring himself to finish the sentence.

"A mermaid, yes."

He didn't say anything. He'd had girlfriends admit all kinds of things to him before—addictions to drugs, thoughts of bisexuality, even a foot fetish—but this was completely out of his depth. He laughed at the thought. Stupid pun.

"Is something funny?"

"Not really. I'm feeling a little like Tom Hanks' character in *Splash.* Sorry, do you know what that is?"

"Yes, it's a mermaid movie. We do our best to keep aware on what humans are saying and thinking about us."

"Humans," he said. "You really aren't human. Great, not only can't I figure out whom to trust in business, I can't seem to do it in relationships either. Maybe I really don't have the sense God gave a horseshoe crab."

"Actually, merfolk, Oceanides, share a lot of DNA in common with humans. And there is some actual human in my lineage, including the unfortunate husband of Melusine. The stories of men being seduced by mermaids and having children with them is true and has been for centuries. But I don't know any horseshoe crabs, so what makes you say that about them?"

"It was an expression my father used whenever I got into trouble, and most frequently after making a wrong decision."

"Am I a wrong decision?"

"That's not what I meant."

"Are you certain?"

He didn't care that she sounded offended and angry. He was the one in the situation who was kept in the dark. He was the one who had been lied to. Again. "You know what happened to me before I came back to work at The Siren, Lyria. I trusted you. I listened to you and was even considering what you said about being a chef."

"What does my being a mermaid have to do with your being a great cook or loving your work in the kitchen? Just because there was something I wasn't ready to tell you, doesn't mean what we shared wasn't real."

"This is about who you *are*, not what you want to do or what's happened to you in your past."

"And at what point was I supposed to tell you in the five days we've been together?"

He didn't like the reminder of how little time they'd actually been together. It felt longer. He cared more about her in the short time than he could recall ever feeling about a woman. To learn about her this way, to see how she didn't trust him, hurt. And hurt was better channeled into anger.

Before he could come up with a reply she continued, "It really didn't seem to fit in any part of our conversations. 'Here, let me put the sauce on that dish for you. By the way, I'm a mermaid staying here until three days past the full moon because there's a Sea Dragon after me and the power of the sapphire jewel on my bracelet.' It would have been so easy to slip in."

"There's a Sea Dragon after you?"

"Yes, aren't you glad you know?"

He wondered if he sounded as nasty as she did

when he was sarcastic. Apparently their races did have a lot in common. Is that who attacked you on the beach?"

"Attacked us both. That's why the bandage is there. But no, what you saw on the beach was a naiad, one of his minions."

"Minions, great."

"I'm sorry I've shattered some grand belief you had about me, Drew. Not even mermaids are perfect, no matter how lovely the stories make us."

"Some stories make you deadly."

She nodded her agreement. "Very true. Still, I didn't mean for you to find out this way. Please believe me when I tell you it wasn't my intention."

"What was?"

She paused and he didn't like it. "You ask questions as though you really want the truth."

"Of course I do. Why wouldn't I?"

"Weren't you the one who told me what the truth did to you?"

"No. Discovering lies hurt me," he said.

"Learning the truth hurt you."

"Semantics aren't helping. It comes out no matter what, Lyria. It can't be hidden forever."

"I understand this is difficult for you to handle. It doesn't fit well in your world, which is why our worlds have always been better off separate. My ancestors discovered this the hard way. It's good to know I am not so foolish."

"Who said anything about my not being able to handle this? Give me a chance, Lyria. You've just told me the woman I love is a creature I believed to be mythical."

215

"A creature, yes. That is what I am to you."

"That's not fair."

"No, the situation is not fair. I expected to be gone before you had a chance to find out. I intended to be a pleasant memory for you, nothing else."

"Even after all we shared, you never intended to stay?"

* * *

"I considered it, and I wondered, but no, I couldn't see how it would be possible." Since her talk with Angelo on the night of the full moon, she'd been wondering if there might be a way for her to remain with Drew. Impossible dreams, foolish thoughts. "It does not work out well when merfolk and humans try to have lengthy relationships. Haven't you read the stories?"

"Why should stories have any significance to what I feel for you? What I know you feel for me? Didn't you hear what I said a little while ago? I love you."

Damn his stubbornness. Before, it was endearing. Now it was going to be a problem. "Those stories are warnings, Drew, and we should both heed them. I have a Sea Dragon to avoid and a stone with magical properties to keep safe."

"You were going to disappear."

"Yes." The word would have had more impact if tears didn't well in her eyes. She tried to blink them away, but they fell on her cheeks.

"Mermaids cry," he said.

"Apparently," she said. "It's rare."

"When you said you couldn't stay I imagined all

216

sorts of reasons, but nothing even close to this," he said. He turned to her and put his hand on her cheek. "I don't know when I stopped thinking of you as a fling which would end, at the latest, when I left Jersey again, but clearly in the short time we've been together, something important has changed."

"Yes, things have changed and my feelings for you run very deep, but the differences in our circumstances remain. Not to mention all my responsibilities," she said.

"As healer?"

She nodded. "I am the heir of the Stone of Clarity. Assuming Fiero, that's the Sea Dragon doesn't kill me tonight, it is what I will continue doing until there is another to pass it to."

"Sounds important."

She sighed. "It is, I suppose, but it isn't what I would have chosen to do."

"What is?" She looked at him and said nothing. He took her hand. "What would you do if you had the freedom to choose?"

She couldn't answer.

Lyria was familiar with the human expression to have a lump in the throat, but she'd never experienced the sensation until now. Drew's question, asked lovingly and openly, made her realize a horrible truth of her own. She had no idea what she wanted for herself. Since she was a child she knew she would be bonded to the bracelet and the Sone on her 18th birthday and her choices would be guided by it forever.

So she never thought much about—didn't allow herself to think about—what she wanted. Since she could never have it, she spent as much time as she could running from or ignoring her responsibilities whenever possible. It was why she was drawn to the Jersey Shore in the first place. The freedom she sensed there was the opposite of what she felt the night before her birthday ceremony.

Just over ten years had passed since then and only now was she discovering she didn't have an answer for the most important question of all.

"It's not easy," he said. She looked at him, meeting his soft gray eyes and seeing understanding. "Knowing what you really want."

"No, it isn't."

"It's tough when what you think you wanted turns out to be wrong, too."

She said nothing. Had she been wrong about not wanting to be a healer? Could it be both her destiny and her desire?

"I guess we aren't so different after all," she said. "My ability to shift appearance notwithstanding, of course."

"Which makes me think of a question. We showered and swam together and you still had legs. How is that possible?" He winced. "Sorry, was that offensive?"

She managed a small smile. "No. It's a logical curiosity under the circumstances and especially given your mention of the movie. Changing from fins to legs and back again is something I can will to happen. We're shifters."

"Can you do it out of the water?"

"Are you asking to see how I look with fins?"

"I've been curious about you since the day we met. Clearly nothing's changed. Yes, I'd like to see."

218

"I don't need water, but I won't be able to move freely so I'll need a little room."

He slid over on the bed, giving her space. She sat next to him and extended her legs next to his, then took his hand. As he stared, her legs seemed to shimmer and blur and as he watched, they merged together and were covered with scales of silvery blue and green. It was the most beautiful color he'd ever seen.

"That's amazing. Does anything else change other than your legs?"

"My lungs. Here, feel my heart rate." She put his hand on her chest and they sat in silence.

"I can't feel anything."

"Exactly. My heart rate drops and my ability to pull oxygen out of the air changes. At this point, I can breathe on land, but not as well as I could if I were under water."

"So you can swim for long distances, then." She nodded. "Can I touch?" he said, gesturing to her tail.

She looked at him as if he were the one who had suddenly fins. "You want to?"

"Why not? They're lovely. As lovely as your legs," She nodded giving him permission. He traced where her hip would be and stroked down, going with the direction of the scales. She knew weren't rough or slippery, closer in texture to sea glass, soft and delicate. He moved his hand to the place on her stomach where the scales began and stroked from skin to scales marveling at the different textures. Tracing fingers over individual scales, he stroked her in the place where she would have been most sensitive had her legs been present. "Do you feel anything in particular when I do this?"

219

"It's not as sensitive as when I have skin, but I admit it's rather arousing to watch you."

"I've never seen a color quite like this. It reminds me of the water in the Caribbean, but not exactly. I don't have the words to describe it."

She tried to say something, then stopped.

"What's wrong?"

"Nothing, exactly. I don't think I've ever felt more vulnerable or more beautiful than I do at this moment."

"You are so much more than beautiful, Lyria. You are magnificent, inside and out."

"Even though I lied to you?"

"I can't believe I'm saying this, but yes. Your lie came from a very understandable fear. It wasn't malice or greed. I can understand your intentions."

"And I can understand your anger."

"Then once again we have more in common than we thought."

"I cannot even begin to fathom how we could make this work." He pulled her close, wrapping a leg around her, embracing her in her shifted form. Her heart filled with emotion she wasn't ready to share but was beginning to accept.

"First things first—we have to find your cousin."

A coldness went through her. "The option of going with the naiad is out."

"Yes, you took care of him rather effectively."

"The Sea Dragon won't hurt her because without her he has no bargaining position. I don't want to try to find or go to him."

"Which leaves him coming to you."

"That's it, Drew. I'll make him come to me."

Something you are doing or thinking is sending out a stronger signal than usual. Lyria remembered Amina's words before giving her the potion. She never remembered to take it, but now she was certain of what needed to happen to allow Fiero to find her and being unshielded was key.

"You have a plan?"

"Absolutely. And you are going to like it." She shifted back to her legs and said, "Kiss me."

"Are you sure?"

Instead of answering, she kissed him, opening his mouth with her tongue. It didn't take long before he was hard, but she added to his desire by stroking his cock and pulling him on top of her.

"I'm not sure my balance is going to be very good with this injury."

"I'm going to take care of that," she said, sliding the head of his cock against her already wet pussy.

"I can't think when you do that," he said.

"Don't worry. This is all about feeling, my love." He trailed his kisses down her jaw and to her breasts, sucking deeply on her nipples and biting them lightly until she gasped and her fluids ran over both of them.

"I don't have anything with me for protection."

"It's not an issue, never has been. I am not fertile this week."

"You know your body well."

"Almost as well as you do," she said as she opened her legs. He pressed his cock against her opening. She didn't let him enter her immediately. Instead she teased them both, using him to stimulate her clit. "Touching you drives me crazy."

"Still more we have in common."

221

Looking into his beautiful gray eyes, she saw every emotion reflected. There was no need to focus her senses on him. She knew how he felt about her, and how much she cared for him. Pulling him on top of her, she spread her legs and brought him into her.

The feel of him stretching her excited her as it always did. It was as if he touched every part of her.

"God, I didn't think being with you could feel any better, but to be naked like this…"

"I'm glad. I so want to be closer to you, as close as possible."

He caressed her body, driving her mad with pleasure and sensation. When he found the rhythm which made her cry out, he placed a hand between them and rubbed her clit, turning her cries to moans.

As her orgasm raced through her, she opened herself up completely to him, the passion and all the emotion she felt for him. And at the same time, she reached out to heal the wound on his leg. Picturing the Stone and sending its power to flow over them both, she sensed the heat and electricity, not needing to look at the bracelet to know it was glowing.

"What's happening?"

"I'm connecting us to the power in the Stone. I'm healing you, healing us.

She raked her nails down his back, marking him, wanting to be as close to him as possible—then even closer. Every concern of connecting with someone, of being known and cared for, even loss came crashing down in the face of a desire greater than any fear she held.

I love you, she thought. When she caught her breath, she said it out loud.

"I love you, too, my beautiful sea goddess." His kiss told her every word was true. Even knowing what she was, who she was he loved her, completely and deeply.

He rolled to the side and pulled her with him. She held him tightly, pressing him against her entire body, wanting to brand the feeling onto her skin.

"I hate to ask," he said, "but now what.

"I don't think we are going to have to wait long for a visit from Fiero."

Sure enough, minutes later the bellow of the Sea Dragon shook the walls. "Come to me now, mermaid."

Drew shot up and put an arm over Lyria.

"I appreciate the cover, my love, but I don't think it's going to do a lot of good," she said.

"Are you really going out there to face him?"

"I must. One way or the other I will be free of him," she said.

"Do you have any idea what you are going to do?"

"I am going to trust." She kissed him deeply, doing what she could to pour her love into him, knowing he would keep it safe. "I hope you will do the same."

* * *

She walked naked onto the beach. Fiero was in human form, standing a few feet back in the water. "So you have accepted you cannot run from me."

"I have accepted that I have no need to. Where is Amina?"

"She is safe and will remain so as long as you do

223

what I ask. Bind yourself to me. Honor the contract your father signed."

"I will do no such thing."

"Then Amina dies."

"In which case I have nothing to lose and you can no longer threaten me."

"You only wish it were that simple. What about the male in your bed? Don't you care for his life?"

"A human male? You must be joking. You and I both know the stories and the truth. Nothing good ever comes of mating with them. They are toys for our fun, nothing else."

"You were right, Wilmar. She does seem cold."

"I would never lie to you, my lord," said a familiar voice. "You know how much your victory matters to me."

Lyria turned to see her former lover sitting comfortably on a rock. She hadn't noticed him, her focus on the real threat.

"I am not convinced it is my victory or her downfall which matters more to you, but that is of no concern."

"Wilmar, I can't believe you would do this?" Lyria asked.

"Do what? Ally myself with the strongest power in the seas?"

"Turn against your people."

"As you turned them against me," Wilmar said.

"I did no such thing. You own foolish pride and ambition did that."

"We will see who the fool is." Wilmar reached an arm out in the direction of the house and moments later Drew appeared, walking toward them as if in a trance. When he reached Wilmar, the merman held a bone knife to his throat.

* * *

"Leave him out of this," she yelled and Drew saw her try to lunge for the merman, but the Sea Dragon threw out something that looked like a net made of light. It wrapped around her legs and pinned her to the spot.

"I think you were wrong about our little mermaid. It would seem she cares a great deal for this simple man. Can't you feel it?" Fiero said. "It must have been something about you she didn't like. I don't think she's as cold as you made her out to be. It will be fun to see if I can warm her in my bed.

"I will never be yours," Lyria yelled.

"You and the Stone will come to me or everyone you love will perish."

"You are the one in danger of great loss. Leave now and you have my assurance we will not hunt you down and destroy you."

"Destroy me? How completely ridiculous."

Drew watched as the man called Fiero shifted his lower half into dragon form, and walked out of the water toward Lyria like a horrifying centaur. He had no idea how or if he could help her, but he stood silently waiting for his chance to be free of the merman who held the blade to his throat.

"You and your kind will kneel before me. If you are a good wife, I will spare those who are important to you. Otherwise at least one a day will die. Beginning with your precious cousin."

The hairs on the back of Drew's neck stood up as

he sensed energy swirling around them. He saw something growing in Lyria's hands, a ball of power. She raised it and threw it at the Sea Dragon, who was caught unprepared. It hit him in the chest and knocked him back, but it wasn't a mortal blow.

"I will confine you, my pretty, just like your ancestor. Never again will you know a breath of freedom." He shot a jolt of what Drew assumed was magic toward Lyria and before he could yell out, she was covered in an eerie light. When it faded she fell to the ground, her body transformed, her legs gone.

"Lyria," Drew cried. She was gasping for air. "What have you done to her?"

"I've taken away her ability to shift at will. She will remain in this form as long as I wish and have legs only when I want her too. Should she try to change on her own, she will die."

Terror coursed through Drew. He wouldn't stand by and watch her die. It didn't matter whether or not they had a future together, as long as she had a future. He had to help.

Remembering every fight he'd had with Michael or Nico, and the effective—and sometimes dirty— tricks they taught him, Drew dropped to the ground and out of Wilmar's grip. He turned around and came up suddenly, slamming the top of his head into the other man's jaw. Unprepared for the attack, Wilmar dropped the knife as he stumbled back. Drew grabbed it, bent over, and sliced the man behind the knees, through tendons that as a swimmer he knew were vital for the body's ability to stand. Before Wilmar could hit the ground, Drew ran over to Lyria.

"No, my love, no. You cannot die. Fight this.

Fight him." He pulled her to him, wishing he could breathe for her.

I can't. He heard her voice in his mind. I wasn't a good sign. She was heavier in this form, but the weight didn't matter. Grabbing her under her arms, he lifted her to face the Sea Dragon.

Standing behind her, letting her body lean against his, he said, "I'm here, Lyria. You can do this." Not knowing why he was doing it, he took her hand and placed it on the mermaid charm he had given her and Stone of Clarity. "We're together. Trust yourself. I love you."

She entwined her fingers with his. *I love you, too.*

No sooner was the thought complete than a blinding light burst through their fingers and heat blazed from the stone. His mind screamed to let go, but he couldn't. Power coursed through them both and the weight of her body eased as her tail shifted back to legs. He didn't understand what was happening, but she stood to face the Sea Dragon, never letting go of his hand. He felt her thoughts leave and stretch out. He didn't know what she was doing until he heard her call,

Amina? Where are you? She paused between each question waiting for a response. *Can you hear me?*

I can.

It was amazing to be part of her thoughts.

Are you safe?

Yes, but how are you doing this? I am too far away and have taken Nerine's potion. This shouldn't be possible.

You would be amazed at what I have discovered is possible. The Stone of Clarity has given me a gift. Fiero claimed he captured you. He had your necklace.

227

It was lost when I was almost abducted. The Stone gave you a gift?

I will explain at another time, just know that I am safe and have nothing to fear from the Sea Dragon any more. Stay where you are and let me know if you need me.

I will. Be well.

And you.

Lyria took a deep breath and brought her awareness back to the beach, the power of the stone still surrounding them both. "You lied. You never had Amina. She is safely hidden from you, and the Stone on my band will never be yours either," she said in a voice filled with power and certainty. Drew thought he'd never heard anything so beautiful.

"This cannot be possible," Fiero said.

"It is more than possible. This is true Clarity. The Stone is mine. By my love and by my trust it is bound to me and answers only to me until such time as I offer it to another of my free will or I die. Its gifts are completely beyond you now, Dragon. But you are not beyond me."

Shock registered clearly on his face. "How dare you? You have no idea what you are talking about. I can and will find the other two and when I do, I will compel you and the Stone of Clarity to obey me."

"Do not threaten me, monster. You have no idea what I, and those who keep the other stones safe, am capable of. And be very careful. There are those close to you who would betray you for their own desires."

"This is far from over, mermaid. I will have what I want one way or the other. There are many willing to help me. The power of the Stone may be yours for now, but your suffering is only beginning."

With a flash of energy Drew was beginning to recognize as magic, the creature sent out an explosion of magic, then shifted fully into dragon form and disappeared.

When Fiero was gone, the light from the Stone faded and Lyria sagged against him. Only then did he feel the pain. "Lyria, something isn't right," he said. Looking down he saw his chest was covered in blood.

* * *

"No," Lyria screamed as Drew fell to the sand. How could he have been hurt without her realizing it? Blood was everywhere. She placed her hands over his heart, feeling its irregular beat. "Don't leave me, Drew. I can't do this without you."

"You can, my beauty. You are capable of so very much. You are such a gift."

"But I want you with me."

"Oh sure," he said with a weak laugh. "Now you realize you can't live without me. I wish I could stay, but I don't think it's possible. Will you go back to Jersey and tell my dad and Mr. V.?"

Her heart was breaking. "I love you. Those words are so small, but I need them to be enough to let you know how much you mean to me. How you have changed me."

"I know, my love," he said, running a hand through her hair.

She could not lose him, not when she finally found love and he found so much to live for as well. She tried to clear her head, to think of something to do, but she was crying too hard.

A tear hit the Stone of Clarity and the gem once again began to glow.

Looking down, she looked the mermaid charm he gave her and this time she was certain it moved. The arm holding the tiny gem reached out and touched the Stone, making it shine brighter.

And the answer came to her. She could feel it. "Did you mean what you said before? Do you want to stay with me?"

"Absolutely. I will gladly be with you until my dying breath, which I don't think is very far off. I'm so glad you came into my life. I love you."

"That's all I needed to know, because your dying breath is not coming for quite some time. Much longer than you realize."

She placed one hand on his wound and another hand on the stone. Instantly, images of him among the merfolk flashed through her mind along with a vision of The Siren filled with Oceanide patrons. Never had she witnessed something so beautiful, something so filled with happiness and love and possibility.

Once again, she opened up her heart to him while also opening to her healing gifts, accepting them completely. Energy and magic flowed from her into him. She opened her eyes when his hand covered hers. The stormy gray of his gaze brought a smile to her lips and tears, this time of joy, to her eyes.

"Take my gift," she said. "Be with me."

As she watched his wound close and sensed his heartbeat grow stronger, she fully accepted her destiny was with this man and his love.

Together they could change the ending of the legends forever.

Epilogue

Six months later

Drew and Lyria lay naked on the beach of their island home. "This is what I call a honeymoon," he said.

"We could go anywhere," she said. "The world is ours to enjoy."

"For now I want to enjoy you here, where we can be alone."

"Sounds perfect to me."

Drew had adjusted to life as a merman as easily as she hoped, given the images of her vision and his preexisting love of swimming. After explaining their sudden and alarming disappearance to the staff at The Siren—Lyria had an emergency and Drew insisted on coming, but hadn't charged his phone—she was welcomed and accepted as a permanent member of the family. Everyone in Lyria's life was happy about her new love and her new commitment to her healer responsibilities. Once she opened herself up, Lyria was thrilled to learn there were many who wanted to be her friend and asked for nothing more than her friendship in return.

There were still times when she was overwhelmed

by how much emotion was a part of her life, and had been since meeting Drew. The day she saved Drew was one of the most powerful in her life.

Wilmar was found crawling through the sand, bleeding from the wound Drew had given him. His punishment was to be healed only to a point—he'd limp badly from now on—and imprisoned in the darkest part of the ocean for the rest of his existence, locked away and unable to harm anyone.

It had only been a few more weeks before all three Stones were safe and the threat to the Oceanides defeated. That had been a frightening and intense time and Lyria was grateful it was behind them.

For the rest of the summer, Drew and Lyria spend a good deal of their time on land since The Siren was busier than ever. Angelo came back to handle the operations side of things which freed Drew to manage the kitchen although he expanded the staff so he could concentrate on creating the specials that were beginning to earn the restaurant rave reviews. In their free time, Lyria helped him adjust to shifting his form, although as someone who'd enjoyed swimming for so much of his life, it wasn't much of a challenge.

Turning over to kiss her, he said, "Did I tell you I completely understand your aversion to clothes, especially underwear?"

"Did I tell you I love that you no longer wear it?"

"I don't know if you've told me, but you've certainly shown me plenty of times."

"I'll probably keep showing you, if you don't mind."

"Not in the least," he said, caressing her breasts and moving down to the juncture between her legs.

She couldn't believe how far they'd come in such a short time. So much had changed, yet so little. Her original home was being expanded so there was more space for them when they resided here and, using the gems and gold that were her inheritance as healer, they moved into a beautiful beach home in Jersey as well. And even though she could have frozen custard and zeppoles whenever she wanted, she still enjoyed every bite of them. Lyria accepted her role as a healer as Drew did his love of cooking. There was no need to keep looking for what made them happy—they already had it.

Drew's relationship with his father continued to improve to the point where he asked if Sam would stand by his side at his fall wedding to Lyria. Everyone was teary after that request. Sam was getting treatments for his cancer and while the doctors were amazed at the improvement he was making, neither Drew nor Lyria were surprised. Each time she saw Sam, she poured a little healing magic into him to help his progress. She would not let Drew lose his father now that he'd finally connected with him. So far Drew and Michael weren't much closer, but Michael had been dumped by Heather and now that the two could commiserate about that, Lyria had hope.

In fact, she had more than hope. She had Drew. Because of him, she discovered her passion and purpose and she'd come to accept her own worthiness and sense of belonging. With him she had discovered love and trust.

And after they made love in the warm afternoon sun, she had a surprise about the future she couldn't wait to share with him.

Keep reading for an excerpt from the next book in the Melusine's Daughters series

Waves of Desire

Chapter One

Present Day

There was a naked woman sunning herself.

One of the things Jonathan Barrett liked most about his morning jog on the beach was that it was one of the only times of the day he wasn't around people. His job as head of security at the Suadela Resort and Spa meant full days of talking, interacting with guests and worrying about their problems. Early morning was his solace from people.

But this morning there was someone else enjoying the sun and solitude. At first he wasn't certain what he was seeing, perhaps it was a trick of the light. As he got closer, however, he was certain it was a person and as he got closer still it was clear he'd come across a nude woman. It seemed wrong to disturb her, after all there was no one else around this early in the morning—most guests slept in after a long night of dancing, partying and hooking up—and she certainly wasn't bothering him.

The beach, which was leased to the resort, was dotted with furniture, some in groups, some alone.

There were cabanas for privacy and those wanting extra amenities like televisions, and lounge chairs open to the sun for comfort, some arranged around fire pits which were lit in the evenings. For their more adventurous and outgoing guests, there were four poster canopied beds. Public acts of sex weren't permitted, but almost everything else was.

Nudity on the beach was also not permitted.

Brian, his high school friend and the Rooms Division Manager of the resort, told him this was something guests tried all the time, but wasn't allowed. Yet. The resort hoped to get a permit for it in the future and if they allowed it prior to going through all the proper legal—and likely illegal—channels, getting the license could be put in jeopardy. Jonathan usually didn't believe in making exceptions, but the beautiful woman with the long red-gold hair deserved to be one.

She was exceptional. The closer he got the more details he noticed. In addition to her beautiful wavy hair, she had long arms and legs and he could detect the outline of muscles, even in her relaxed position, which mean she was in very good shape. He estimated she was probably about 5'8", maybe a little taller, and he couldn't help but think how well that could fit against his 6'1" frame. A lot of his friends preferred petite women, but he'd always had a thing for taller ones. Her fingers were clear of nail polish and she had an astonishing natural beauty about her. All he could see that adorned her was a thin gold chain around her waist, accenting how small it was, how nicely her hips flared out.

Damn, she was sexy. Her hair was pulled back

but he could see it was a reddish blonde. Her waist was small, her hips curvy, and her breasts were gorgeous, and clearly natural. Everything about her was appealing. Arousing.

But she wasn't allowed to be out naked on resort property.

When he was closer he heard her humming. He didn't recognize the song, but it was beautiful. Clearing his throat and hoping not to startle her he said "Excuse me, miss, but this isn't a nude beach." There was no response so he walked a little closer. "I don't mean to bother you, but even though it's early, you're not permitted to sunbathe naked on this property."

She took a deep breath which raised her breasts, but other than that she gave no acknowledgement she'd heard him. As he walked closer he saw she was lightly tan all over, no lines to mar the perfection of her skin. Either she'd found the best tanning salon in the world, or she regularly laid out in the sun naked. Something told him it was the latter.

Finally, he was close enough to cast a shadow over her face. She turned to him and opened her eyes. He was momentarily dazzled by their deep green color.

"You can't sunbathe naked here."

"I'm not naked," she said in a soft, sexy voice that sounded as though she'd just woken from a wonderful dream. "I'm wearing this." She held out her right arm which he couldn't see before and the sunlight caught the facets of the jewels in her bracelet. It was gorgeous. Heavy but delicate at the same time and like nothing he'd ever seen before.

"I don't think that counts."

"Too bad," she said sitting up and turning toward him. She looked at him closely and he felt frozen by her gaze. Her body was luscious and stunning but in the moment all he could do was look into her eyes. Fathomless, and the color was like nothing he'd never seen outside of a painting or something computer generated.

He didn't know how long she stared at him before she said, "Pain. Loneliness. That's too bad. I am so sorry."

Before he could come up with a response to her disturbing summary of him, she shifted to sitting on her knees. Then she raised herself up so they were facing each other and put her arms around him then kissed him full on the mouth.

There was nothing hesitant about her touch. One moment she was looking at him and seeing into his emotions, the next she was pressed against him, clearly not caring that she was naked or that he was fully dressed.

His arms moved of their own accord and wrapped around her body and he pulled her closer to him so he could feel the heat of her skin through his shirt. He was instantly hard. He couldn't remember reacting to a woman this fast since he was in high school and had no control over his body's responses. But this reaction, although fast as those early days—if not faster—was different. Something in him cracked. Something in him wanted to open up and drink her in completely.

The feel of her mouth and now her tongue was beyond intoxicating. She tasted of salt and sea, of sunshine and something elusive and desirable.

How could anyone kiss like this? He felt

completely drunk and instantly sober. Aware of every muscle in his body, the air around him blowing over his skin, and yet his only focus was her. His will, his thoughts, disappeared. This is what it meant to be captivated by someone. For some reason it wasn't as upsetting as he ever thought it would be.

He'd had plenty of women throw themselves at him in the years since he started working at the resort. On occasion, when it had been too long, he'd taken them up on the offer, but more often he passed. He'd learned that quickie sex was no more satisfying that fast food. Fine in the moment, followed hours of regret after. Not worth it

But this? Now? Her? Was completely different.

He kept trying to remind himself a woman he'd just met, whose name he didn't know was draped over him, but the feel of her hands raking through his hair had his blood boiling and logic didn't stand a chance.

He wanted more. He moved his mouth away from hers touch more of her, starting at her jaw and then moving toward her neck. At the hollow at the base of her throat he licked her, wanting to learn the taste of her skin, aching to know where she wanted to be touched, what excited her.

Her head fell back as he worked his way down to her breasts. They overflowed his hands, the nipples hard and responsive. He latched his mouth onto one as his fingers rolled the sensitive tip of the other and his blood surged as she moaned and pushed herself more into his mouth.

His fingers traced the sensitive skin between her breasts and he lifted one so that he could lick the skin underneath. A breeze came in and she shuddered. He could imagine how the cool air felt on her wet heated skin, and knowing he was responsible for her pleasure was a heady feeling.

He touched her everywhere he could has her hands roamed his body, lifting his shirt out of the waistband of his shorts and sliding her fingers underneath to touch his skin. He felt as though he were on fire.

But he wanted more. Needed more.

As if she'd heard his thoughts she pulled him closer and brought him onto the bed with her, moving toward the center so he'd have room next to her.

He'd never known desire like this, didn't know it possible. It slammed into him with a fierceness which would have terrified him under normal circumstances. But this was about as far from normal as it was possible to get.

He had to find out how she tasted. All at once nothing seemed as important. He put one hand behind her back and the other between her breasts and pushed gently. She stopped what she was doing to look at him, then gave him a smile that suggested she loved the way his thoughts worked. She let him guide her until she was again prone on the bed then he removed his hand and went back to kissing her breasts, now moving his way down her stomach.

Her legs unhooked from behind his back and she allowed them to fall open, exposing herself to the sun and to him. His hands traced the sensitive skin of her inner thighs. Her pussy wasn't shaved bare as so many women did and the light coating of hair, the same beautiful light strawberry color as the hair on her head excited him. He gently brushed his fingers through it, enjoying the texture and noticing that at the center, it was damp.

The brightness of the day made the slickness of her skin shine and he stroked a finger from her clit down to the base of her opening and to the beginning of the skin below. He was rewarded with a moan of pleasure and an increase in wetness.

Her natural and uninhibited response was as exciting as everything else he experienced about her. He breathed her in as he tasted her passion for the first time. She arched up and sighed when his tongue touched her and it was all the encouragement he needed.

She tasted of honey and salt and something that was uniquely her. Jonathan loved everything about oral sex, learning what a woman tasted like, what pleased her. It was so fucking amazing.

And this woman was one of the most responsive he'd ever been with. He wanted to devour her—and he did. Using his tongue and his fingers he listened to her responses and intensified the things that made her moan or sigh longer.

Her orgasm was as natural and beautiful as she was. She cried out to a "Goddess" and he continued to please her with his tongue and fingers until her breathing almost returned to normal. She reached out to him and caressed his hair, his shoulders. He kissed his way up her body, loving the warmth of her skin, the taste of her lingering on his tongue.

He kissed her and she pressed herself against his length. Moving to kiss his jaw and then nip at his ear she whispered, "More."

He was on fire for her and couldn't wait to get his

clothes off. His phone rang as he reached for the waist band of his shorts. Not only did the song ruin the mood, but it was Brian's ringtone. If he was calling this early there must be something important he needed Jonathan for.

"I need to take this call, sexy," he told her giving her a kiss. When she reached for him to pull him closer he stepped away. If she touched him again he'd be lost, and Brian could go to hell until they were done.

Done. What a ridiculous thought. He couldn't imagine ever getting enough of her.

"Just give me a minute." Less if that was possible. He intended to make this the shortest phone call in history. "What's up," he said into the phone knowing no other preamble was needed.

"Got a security issue already. Some woman can't get into her room and she thinks her roommate is unconscious inside. Meet me as soon as you can at Room 306. I have a feeling this needs at least two people if not to help, then to keep the stories straight. I think she's still drunk."

Damn, hell and several other emphatic words rushed through Jonathan's mind. What he said instead was, "Okay, I'm on the beach. I'll be up there as soon as I can." He hung up and as he was putting the phone back in his pocket he said, "Sorry to cut this short, but if you'll come to the resort with me I'm sure we can…"

She was gone.

* * *

As soon as his back was turned, Amina silently moved off the bed and into the ocean, transforming her legs into fins immediately and swimming away from the beach. Usually she wasn't so careless around and with humans, but today she'd needed a little time in the sun to rest and think and decide what to do now that Lyria was safely ensconced in some place called New Jersey. She worried about her cousin. Unlike Amina, Lyria never spent time in the human world.

Amina had seen the human resorts along the beaches before and had even taken advantage of the amenities—and men—of several. It was like a buffet of fun. Easy access, lots of choices. This morning, however, she'd wanted rest and quiet. To be away from the noise of the ocean and the restlessness of her thoughts.

And worse her emotions and the near constant barrage of the feelings of others.

She liked to be free to do what she wished when she wished. Lyria was the serious one, the one good at responsibility. Amina wanted to enjoy everything she could while she had the chance. Her empathic abilities and the requirements of Melusine's Band limited her life enough. She worked very hard to keep time to herself for whatever pleasure she deemed desirable at the time. This morning, the human on the beach was quite desirable.

When the man had come upon her she intended to dazzle him, an ability she and other merfolk had to make humans forget what they had seen, then slip away leaving him with the feeling of a mirage or dream. That changed when she looked into his eyes

His pain and passion hit her with the ferocity of a

tidal wave and she couldn't turn away. Usually she could control her abilities, especially around men, but with the intensity of his emotions struck her unexpectedly and quickly. All at once she could feel the ache and anger he carried around with him. As if that wasn't enough, beneath the violent emotions was a pent up hunger and need for connection she doubted he was aware of on any conscious level.

It was a need she understood profoundly, although not one she shared with anyone.

It wasn't any hardship to kiss him. She'd kissed many humans in her time although generally, and unlike some merfolk, she wasn't attracted to them for any length of time. She found most of them to be boring and completely unaware of the vastness of the world they lived in. If they could have seen a fraction of what she had, they would be different. They were fun to flirt with and occasionally enjoy for pleasure, but no more than that.

But something in her was drawn to this human and she wanted to know how his lips would feel on hers.

Surprisingly, as soon as they touched something exciting and dangerous filled her with a yearning and she deepened the kiss immediately, making it clear to him that she was interested in more. She tasted his hesitation along with the salt of his skin and a hint of toothpaste but that lasted only for a moment before he leaned forward and put his arms around her, drawing her close.

It had been a long time since Amina indulged herself with a man, human or merfolk. Along with her cousin most of the last year she'd been worried about

Fiero, the sea dragon who was after the power in the three of Melusine's bands, and her time and efforts were taken up with trying to figure out where he was and what he planned to do to acquire the bracelets and the women who wore them. These concerns along with her regular duties as a counsellor gave her less free time than usual. Her empathic abilities gave her a unique take on the position and she was often called in to high government meetings at home and with other communities because of her skills.

But she didn't think it was abstinence that caused her to invite this man into her body. It also wasn't only because he was exactly the type of man she found attractive. What was it the human books said? Tall, dark, and handsome. He was clearly taller than her by a few inches and given that he lived on this island the tan was no surprise. But oh, was he handsome.

He was gorgeous and fit with dark hair that looked like it got in his eyes on occasion and brown eyes so dark they were almost black. The sheen of perspiration and rapid breathing from his run only made him sexier. From the stubble on his jaw she knew he hadn't shaved yet that morning, and there was a thin scar on the center of his check about an inch below his eye. He could have lost sight in it had the cut that caused the scar been any higher.

It was when she looked into his eyes that she was lost. Immediately she had flashes of violence and pain, both his and others followed immediately by terrible sadness and regret. She could hardly believe that a man with such intense emotions coursing through him could manage to look calm. She wondered if he knew how much pain he was in. It was the desire to alleviate his pain—not his incredibly kissable lips, honestly—which made her pull him onto the bed with her.

Once she touched him all other thoughts fled and she let her body take the lead. It wasn't long before he had brought her to a breathless, crashing orgasm. She couldn't remember the last time she'd experienced pleasure like that, and she certainly had never indulged in so much with a man she'd just met. Or with a human. Whose name she didn't even know.

Her shamelessness washed over her when he was on the phone and she was grateful he wasn't looking at her and couldn't see her blush. She may have always had a light tan, but her fair complexion made her rosy from top to tail when she was embarrassed. While he was focused elsewhere, she slipped off the rock and swum out to sea.

Amina put distance between herself and the beach, but she could still see him and had to admit to herself she wanted to see his reaction when he turned his attention back to her. Her eyesight was much stronger than that of a human's since she needed to see clearly underwater. She was more than a mile away but could read him without a problem. His body language told her he was confused, upset and then disappointed. She hated adding more negative emotions to the man's life, but it couldn't be helped. And although she was also a touch pleased at his frustration, this was the wrong time for her to be involved with anyone.

Especially a human.

About the Author

A Jersey Girl trapped without good diners or boardwalks in New England, Rachel Kenley is a novelist, workshop leader, and co-founder of the Writers Business School (www.writersbusinessschool.com). She speaks nationally on writing, business, and how to connect with your heart's desire.

Rachel's first romance novel was published in 2007 when the e-book world was new. Since then she has had seven novels and numerous short stories and novellas released, with many reaching her publishers bestseller lists. She is a member of the International Women's Writers Guild, Essex Writers and Artisans Guild, the Vice President of Broad Universe, and Vice President for Events of the Independent Publishers of New England.

When she is not writing Rachel is homeschooling her sons, trying unsuccessfully to keep up with laundry, and laughing as much as possible. She believes in shameless flirting, never missing the chance to watch *The Wizard of Oz* and the emotional and economic power of retail therapy. Please don't talk to her before her morning cup of coffee.

Rachel can be found on Facebook at www.facebook.com/authorrachelkenley and on the web at www.rachelkenley.net—where there's a free story download and other treats, so come visit!

If you liked this, you might like these other titles from Riverdale Avenue Books

By Rachel Kenley:

Her Beastly Stepbrother:
A Once Upon a Stepbrother Novella

Her Stepbrother's Christmas Gift:
A Once Upon a Stepbrother Novella

Her Frozen Stepbrother
A Once Upon a Stepbrother Novella

Her Stepbrother, The Wolf

The Glass Stiletto
A BDSM Fairy Tale

And:

Her Stepbrothers' Demands
By Trinity Blacio

Her Stepbrothers are Aliens
By Trinity Blacio

Her Stepbrothers are Demons
By Trinity Blacio

Her Stepbrothers are Blood Suckers
By Trinity Blacio

Her Stepbrothers are Angels
By Trinity Blacio

Her Stepbrothers are Saber Tooth Tigers
Book Five of the Masters of the Cats Series
By Trinity Blacio

Trinity Blacio's Paranormal Stepbrothers Omnibus:
Volume One
By Trinity Blacio

The Red Shoes
By John Stewart Wynne